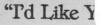

## "I'd Like Y

she said, her voice whispery soft.

She wanted this man who thrilled her, who had probably known a hundred women. Whatever the past had been, whatever the future might be, she wanted this night with him. He had tantalized her with a glimpse of what could be between a man and a woman. She wanted to know it all. She had waited too long for that knowledge.

As he closed the door behind them, Theo said tentatively, "Toni, I . . ."

"No, don't say anything," she answered. Then, with a slow, shy smile spreading across her face, she finished, "I think the time for talk is past."

## PAMELA WALLACE

creates spirited characters that come alive on every page as she weaves a thought-provoking story of "real" love and romance. Ms. Wallace lives in Fresno, California. This is her first Silhouette Desire.

Dear Reader:

SILHOUETTE DESIRE is an exciting new line of contemporary romances from Silhouette Books. During the past year, many Silhouette readers have written in telling us what other types of stories they'd like to read from Silhouette, and we've kept these comments and suggestions in mind in developing SILHOUETTE DESIRE.

DESIREs feature all of the elements you like to see in a romance, plus a more sensual, provocative story. So if you want to experience all the excitement, passion and joy of falling in love, then SILHOUETTE DESIRE is for you.

I hope you enjoy this book and all the wonderful stories to come from SILHOUETTE DESIRE. I'd appreciate any thoughts you'd like to share with us on new SILHOUETTE DESIRE, and I invite you to write to us at the address below:

Karen Solem
Editor-in-Chief
Silhouette Books
P.O. Box 769
New York, N.Y. 10019

# PAMELA WALLACE
## Come Back, My Love

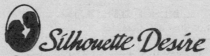

*Silhouette Desire*

Published by Silhouette Books New York

**America's Publisher of Contemporary Romance**

SILHOUETTE BOOKS, a Simon & Schuster Division of
GULF & WESTERN CORPORATION
1230 Avenue of the Americas, New York, N.Y. 10020

ISBN: 0-671-45064-6

First Silhouette Books printing August, 1982

10 9 8 7 6 5 4 3 2 1

*To Elnora King,*
*who is always right*

# 1

~~~~~~~~~~~~~~~~~~~~~

**A**ntonia Lawrence watched carefully, her body tense and her gaze shrewdly calculating, as the wave crested just in front of her. It was taller than she and a miscalculation could send her battered and breathless to the ocean floor. A split second before the massive wave broke, she dove into it, slicing through the water and coming up behind the stormy, pounding foam. Treading water, she watched as the wave spent itself on the shore.

Though it was growing late and she was beginning to feel the icy cold, Toni threw herself into the waves again and again. Finally, when her tiny body was spent, she rode a wave back to the beach. Picking up a thick, heavy towel that she had dropped on the dry sand earlier, she continued up the beach, toweling herself dry and shivering in the crisp, cool October air.

It was late afternoon, and the sun was setting spectacularly over the horizon. The sky was slashed with broad strokes of flaming red, burnt orange and deep gold, while the sun itself was a sliver of darker orange on the edge of the horizon.

The fading sunlight was behind Toni as she strode up

the beach, and it lit her vividly—her warm, peaches-and-cream complexion; her deep gentian-violet eyes that shone now with a luminous intensity. Her hair, the wet, curling tendrils framing her fragile-looking, elfin face, was like a halo on fire. The color was a breathtakingly, unabashedly Titian red-gold that made a shiny new copper penny seem dull in comparison. As Toni passed people on the beach, they turned to look at the fiery mass of irrepressible curls that hugged her head like flames enveloping the head of a match.

"What are you trying to do? Take on the entire Pacific Ocean?"

The tone was mocking but the speaker, a young woman who was sitting on the brick patio of Toni's Malibu beach house, was grinning good-naturedly. Small like Toni, but more inclined to plumpness, she had almond-shaped hazel eyes that seemed continually amused. Her chestnut-brown hair hung thick and straight past her shoulders, pulled back from her heart-shaped face by a tortoise-shell band.

Toni said nothing as she pulled on a terrycloth cover-up in a deep burgundy shade. Then she sank gratefully onto a yellow-cushioned, wrought-iron chair. Curling her bare feet under her, she sighed deeply. There was exhaustion in the sound, and something else, a longing, a frustration. Though she was no longer shivering with cold and she should have been able to relax, her heart continued to beat frantically, and her whole being was suffused with an electricity, an intensity. It made her wide, deep-set eyes look almost black instead of violet, and her full lower lip trembled slightly as if she could barely contain her anger.

Watching her carefully, Carol pushed a plate of Brie and crisp crackers toward Toni on the yellow-cloth-covered table.

"Have something to eat. You must be famished. Just watching you has made me hungry."

"No, thanks," Toni said curtly. Her voice was surprisingly low and husky for such a petite young woman; there was nothing little-girlish about it.

"How about some wine, then?" Carol offered, pouring Toni a glass.

"No."

Clearly trying to make conversation, Carol said brightly, "By the way, the Prince and Princess of Wales were in the news again. She's pregnant. You know, when we were covering the wedding, I thought she looked like the terribly fertile sort. Bound to have lots of little princes and princesses."

Toni looked out at the ocean, but her thoughts weren't on the sandpipers mincing along the shore, or the oil tanker on the horizon. She was remembering what had happened when she and Carol covered the royal wedding for a local L.A. television station . . . and the night that began with a date with a stranger and ended with a carriage ride through Hyde Park with a lover. . . .

Shifting her slender legs restlessly, Toni drummed nervously on the arm of the chair with slender, porcelain-smooth hands.

"Hey, what's wrong, Toni? You look like you could chew nails."

"Nothing," Toni responded firmly, but her tone clearly indicated that *everything* was wrong.

"Okay," Carol replied, drawing out the word slowly. Then she continued bluntly, "But I haven't seen you look so unsettled since your divorce."

"Look, it's been a hectic week," Toni insisted, her words clipped to the point of rudeness. "I'm just *tired.*"

"Fine," Carol agreed easily, knowing Toni too well to be baited by her explosive but short-lived temper. "But I don't understand why you close up every time someone mentions anything connected with the royal wedding. Or why you've been thoroughly disagreeable to just about everyone for weeks now."

"Carol . . ."

"No, listen to me," Carol interrupted firmly. "You haven't been yourself lately, and you know it. Something has happened to change you. And I've got to say, you don't look *tired*. You look . . ." She paused, searching for the right word. Scrutinizing Toni carefully, her pale eyes narrowing in speculation, she went on, "Come to think of it, I don't think I've ever seen you look quite this way. Lit up like a Christmas tree but kind of edgy somehow. Angry yet excited. If I didn't know you better, I'd say . . ."

Carol stopped, thunderstruck by the sudden realization that had just hit her. "Toni! You met a guy, didn't you? In London!"

"*Carol,*" Toni began hotly. Suddenly the fury that had been growing steadily for two months erupted into laughter; uninhibited, wholehearted laughter at the absurdity of the situation and at herself for being such a fool.

"I'm sorry," she finally managed to say, wiping tears from her eyes. "It's just that I realized what a fool I've been. I've no right to take it out on the rest of the world just because he never called. And besides, I *did* tell him not to call. I knew it was a fling, nothing permanent, and I didn't want to be awkward about it. But still, I *expected* to hear from him by now."

She was babbling and she knew it, but she didn't know how to stop. Somehow, Carol seemed to understand it all.

"Antonia Marie Lawrence, it isn't in your nature to have a *fling,* and you know it. You're in *love.* If it happened that fast, in just a few days in London, then you must be head over heels in love!"

"Oh, but, Carol, I *can't* be. I *won't* be. I don't *want* to be. After Robert made such a fool of me, I swore it would never happen again. I'm so *mad* at myself!"

"I know," Carol laughed happily. "But I never expected you to stick to that cloistered nun routine. After all, you were reading Emily Dickinson in college while the rest of us were practicing 'free love.' Face it, girl, you're an incurable romantic."

She added drily, "I've always thought you missed your century somehow. You should have been born in a time when knights in shining armor swept innocent damsels off their feet and onto white steeds. Even after the divorce, I don't think you entirely got it through your head that people don't live happily ever after anymore."

"Well, Theodopolus Chakiris is definitely *not* a knight in shining armor. And there won't be any 'ever after.'"

"In that case, accept it for what it was—a wonderful interlude with no strings attached. Be practical for once in your life. Don't expect more. Nowadays love has to be taken where and when it comes along. And romance is a guy who stops to kiss you before walking out the door."

Toni laughed in spite of herself at Carol's down-to-earth advice. She knew that Carol practiced what she preached, contenting herself with one noncommittal affair after another. Carol didn't expect Mr. Right to come along, and therefore wasn't disappointed when he didn't show.

"Look at it this way," Carol continued. "You went to London, which is a storybook place to begin with, and covered the wedding of a prince, which is right out of any book of fairy tales. Naturally, you were caught up in the rampant romance. Think of it—the cavalry with their shining breastplates, the million-dollar wedding in a cathedral, all of that magnificent spectacle. Even the Archbishop of Canterbury called it 'the stuff of which fairy tales are made.' It's no wonder that you were carried away."

"But I should have known better," Toni insisted stubbornly.

"Hey, this is a vulnerable time for you. You've been acting very blasé about the divorce, but I know what a tremendous disappointment it was to you. You gave so much. And to watch it all crumble into dust hurts like hell."

As Toni picked up the glass of cold, sparkling white wine, and sipped it slowly, she carefully considered Carol's harshly realistic words. Is that all it was? she asked herself bluntly, just an emotional response to a highly emotional event? It was true that as she covered the wedding, watching the fantasy unfold, she could not remember a day quite like it.

London was dressed like a vast stage, the quaint double-decker buses painted with wedding bows and the parks blooming with Prince Charles' royal crest outlined in precisely planted blossoms. The frantic pace, the giddy nerves, the spiraling expectations, all led up to a celebration of one of the fundamental functions of human beings, the consummation of love. When Charles claimed his Diana with such pride, such transparent adoration, Toni had felt her eyes fill with tears and her heart become heavy with a poignant mixture of envy and happiness.

*Was* she simply swept away by the storybook splendor of it all? she wondered pensively.

"Who *is* this Chakiris guy, anyway? Anyone I've met?"

Somehow, Toni was reluctant to discuss the hard facts of the encounter, to give a blow-by-blow account of her fall from the carefully structured isolation of her life. The wall had crumbled so unexpectedly, yet so completely. She still wasn't at ease with the realization she'd let someone touch her again. And the fact that she had been touched more deeply than *ever* before only made it worse, like rubbing salt in a still tender wound.

For a month she had tried to keep it a secret. Even now, she could hardly bear to think about it. It embarrassed her terribly and made her feel unaccountably shy.

Perhaps she *had* merely been building castles in the air,

she realized ruefully, and they had inevitably come
tumbling down. Still, she couldn't talk about it objectively, in the cold light of day. Not yet, while she still
remembered vividly how it felt to be held in Theo's arms.

"Just . . . just someone I met," Toni finally answered
hesitantly.

Her reluctance, the depth of her feelings, were obvious. As an old friend, Carol normally would have pressed
for details. This time, she didn't pursue a subject that was
obviously sensitive.

"Well, I'm *glad* it happened," she insisted. "It was just
plain unhealthy the way you were before, refusing to
even date anyone."

Changing the subject rather obviously, but with an
endearing charm, she continued, "And covering the
wedding certainly boosted your career. Barbara Walters,
watch out!"

Laughing, Toni responded drily, *"Sure.* After only two
years as a television reporter, I don't think I'm any threat
to her."

They lapsed into shoptalk then, recalling the events
they had covered in London, Toni as a reporter and
Carol as her producer. It had, indeed, been an exciting
time, filled with endless interviews with everyone from
cockney porters to the designers of Princess Diana's
wedding gown. Toni, Carol and the cameraman and
sound man from station KABN in Los Angeles had little
time to enjoy London as tourists. Instead of visiting the
Tower of London or Harrod's department store, they ran
after scoops and attended endless press briefings.

Toni kept her reminiscences with Carol carefully professional, as they recalled the wildly hectic assignment.

Talking about work kept Toni from dwelling on that
strange, wonderful, tempestuous night with Theo. It kept
her from thinking about the man who brought fire to her
yearning body and love to her empty heart. He made her

feel innocent again, as if at twenty-eight, she'd never even suspected the depth of intimacy that can exist between a man and a woman.

Finally, Carol asked tentatively, "You never heard from him again? The guy you met in London, I mean."

Toni felt her mouth tighten into a frown and she knew there was a flash of irritation in her eyes. She looked directly at Carol. "No. I didn't expect to, really."

"Oh? Well, it's only been a couple of months. Maybe he's still in Europe. I bet you'll hear from him when he gets back to the States."

"Look, Carol," Toni responded firmly, "it didn't last very long. In fact, it was your classic one-night stand, though I don't like to admit it. It's over. *Period.*" She couldn't help adding, "And besides, he made it quite clear how he feels about commitment."

"Oh, I see. . . ." Carol answered, her expression thoughtful. She leaned back in her chair and took another long sip of wine.

Toni brushed aside a still-wet curly strand of hair from her forehead. "What's that supposed to mean?"

"Just 'oh.'" Then, leaning forward and setting her glass down on the table, Carol continued lightly, "Men are all alike, I guess. It's wham, bam, thank you, ma'am."

"Carol, *don't.*"

Carol looked at Toni more intently. "Don't what?"

"Just *don't.* Let's change the subject." Toni leaned back in her chair, no longer interested in the wine or the food.

"He must be pretty important," Carol finally said after a long, tense silence.

Toni didn't respond for a long moment. The fact that she was quietly thoughtful instead of lashing out indignantly was very revealing. "I don't know how important he is. And I never will know. I don't expect to ever see him again. We had one night in London. And that was the end of it."

Her tone was final, yet somehow not truly accepting.

Carol responded gently, "Having been in the same situation myself, so many times, I know that the only answer is time. After awhile, the pain will grow less and less. You'll always wonder what you might have had together if he'd been willing to pursue a relationship. But gradually it will become simply an interesting, hypothetical question, instead of a burning curiosity." Then, pulling herself up and smiling determinedly, she finished, "In the meantime, it's best not to dwell on it. Let's go see a movie. There's a new Robert Redford film playing at the Malibu Cinema. And we could get a pizza afterward."

Toni smiled. "No, thanks. You know, you don't have to treat me like it was my first rejection. I'm okay. It takes more than one devastatingly attractive Greek-American photographer to get me down."

"Okay, champ, I get it. *Down* but not *out*. Would you like to watch television then?"

"No. Actually, if you don't mind, I'd like to turn in early tonight. As you well know, boss, I've got a ton of work to do tomorrow. Do you mind if I kick you out now?"

"Of course not," Carol answered, rising and grabbing her purse. "One for the road," she smiled, taking a handful of crackers. "See you tomorrow, Toni." As Toni started to rise, Carol finished, "No, don't get up. Finish your wine. 'Night."

"Carol . . . I'm sorry I've been so irritable. I appreciate your concern."

"Don't mention it."

A moment later, Toni was alone, with nothing but the distant hum of traffic along Pacific Coast Highway and the occasional squawk of a seagull for company.

When the sun was gone completely and night had fallen, she went into the house. It was small, just one bedroom and bathroom, a tiny kitchen, and a medium-size living room with a dining area at one end. One wall of the living room was covered with floor-to-ceiling

windows that flooded the room with sunlight, making it
bright and cheerful during the day. The entire house was
done in shades of blue and peach. The colors were
repeated on the comfortable chintz sofa and armchairs in
front of the fireplace, and peach paint covered the walls.

The bay-windowed dining area had a double pedestal
table, and chairs upholstered in the same fabric as the
furniture. Antique porcelains were scattered around the
room. The shining hardwood floor was covered by a
lovely dhurrie rug in the dining area patterned in blue
and peach.

The atmosphere was made even more cheerful and
pleasant by fresh flowers—yellow daisies, tiny white
carnations and blue iris—in tall glass vases and round
brass bowls.

Toni gloried in the peaceful atmosphere of the house.
When she left her husband, Robert, taking nothing but
her clothes, she fled to this house as one might flee to a
refuge. It was a gift from her grandmother on her
twenty-first birthday, but she had never actually lived in it
during her troubled marriage. Her husband was a successful, wealthy novelist, and he didn't feel the house was
impressive enough for his lavish lifestyle.

But to Toni, it was a haven. She came here often when
she needed to be alone, to escape the pressure and
unhappiness of her life with Robert. When she left Robert
and moved into the house, she felt as if it had always
been home—unlike the huge, starkly modern Beverly
Hills mansion where she had always felt like just another
of Robert's expensive possessions.

Walking into the kitchen, Toni recorked the half-empty
bottle of wine and placed it in the refrigerator. After
throwing away the remnants of cheese and crackers, she
went into her bedroom.

It was a lovely room, the walls painted a soft seafoam
blue that matched the fabric on an armchair in a corner.
Next to the chair was a small, round table draped with the

same fabric. Piled high on the table were stacks of books and magazines. The Chippendale canopy bed, another gift from her grandmother, was hung with white eyelet.

The mood of the room was romantic, comfortable, cozy.

In the plant-filled, yellow-tiled bathroom, Toni drew a steaming hot bath. Quickly shedding her clothes, she relaxed in the water for a long time, letting the warmth of the water soothe her tired, tense body. She lingered as long as possible, until the water had become tepid. For some reason she was filled with an uncharacteristic lethargy tonight. Normally energetic, she was reluctant now to do anything, even go through the simple routine of preparing for bed.

Finally, she stepped out of the tub, rubbed herself vigorously with a thick towel and slipped on a furry white robe.

In the living room, she built a small fire in the red brick fireplace, then curled up in a corner of the brightly flowered chintz sofa. She was halfway down the page of a novel when she realized that she couldn't remember a word she'd read. Her mind simply wasn't on it.

She thought of Carol's prying questions. No, not prying, she corrected herself. Carol cared about her and merely wondered how important Theo was to her happiness. Toni considered the question carefully. In the two months that had elapsed since that night in London, her life had gone on as usual, at least on the surface. She had worked hard, visited with Carol and other friends, spent one quiet weekend with her grandmother in Santa Barbara.

But always at the back of her mind was the memory of Theo's parting words—"I'll call you." His failure to call, to contact her at all since then, hurt when she let it.

She tried hard not to let it.

Irritated with herself, she put down the book, turned out the light and went to bed.

But in the loneliness of her large bed, she found it hard to go to sleep.

With the house dark and quiet, Toni could no longer avoid the thoughts that she had determinedly driven from her mind for so long.

What did I do? she asked herself angrily.

The answer came as sharp and clear as the ringing of a silver bell—*you fell in love.* And the feeling was unlike anything she had known before, even during the entire five years of her marriage.

But how on earth did it happen? she wondered as she was overwhelmed by a growing drowsiness.

In that netherworld between sleep and wakefulness, she remembered how it happened . . . with fireworks blazing and horns blowing and an almost magical retreat into a fairy-tale world where princes still claimed their princesses. . . .

Toni arched her neck to look up in wonder and excitement at the fireworks being set off over the cavalry parade ground at Hyde Park. It was the eve of the wedding and the huge park was filled with 700,000 people come to watch the most spectacular fireworks display in history. Fiery images of Prince Charles and Lady Diana hung suspended in midair, then were followed in a burst of riotous color by the crests and badges of the prince.

When twenty-five bursts of fireworks were set off within one minute of each other, the vast, milling crowd gasped, then applauded. But the excitement hardly had time to abate before the music of the 350-piece band and the 150-voice choir built to a crescendo, perfectly timed with another burst of dazzling lights in the sky.

For the first time all week, Toni was on her own, not on assignment. Like everyone else there, she came simply because she had never gotten over her childhood awe of brightly colored fire in the sky. It was a perfect night for the dazzling show, cool and clear. As huge as Hyde Park was, it actually seemed cozy as adults and children filled it.

Toni moved happily through the crowd, taking it all in, the myriad sights, the smells, the air of joyous celebration. Love was in the air, and everyone had come to pay homage to it. Somehow, the royal wedding had touched them all, making them stop and think for a moment, rather wistfully, about love, and the part it played in their own lives.

When Toni arrived in London she was determined to be an objective reporter. But her objectivity quickly melted in the face of the overwhelming sense of giddiness at the excitement of it all. Gradually, she was swept up in the infectious high spirits. Now, she didn't even try to resist the rampant happiness.

"There goes another one," a man near her said breathlessly as the sky was filled with a fireworks palace.

The crowd let out a collective sigh of awe, then quieted to a momentary lull while a man was raised 150 feet over the ground in a crane. In the brief stillness, Toni looked at the people surrounding her. There were young lovers lying on blankets, as entranced with each other as with the fireworks; and whole families sitting together, drinking from thermoses of hot tea. Next to Toni, a very pregnant young woman sat placidly, while her son, who couldn't have been more than three, stood close by.

The boy, a short, pudgy figure with glistening blond hair and huge, cornflower-blue eyes, was having a difficult time seeing beyond the adults towering over him. He strained his little neck as far back as it would go, trying to watch the man going up in the crane.

Kneeling beside him, Toni asked softly, "Would you like me to hold you up so you can see better?"

For just a moment the boy held back shyly, then his curiosity got the better of him. He held out his hands for Toni to take him. She looked questioningly at his mother, who said, smiling, "Go ahead. And thanks ever so," in a lovely English accent. Patting her large stomach, she explained unnecessarily, "I'm afraid I'm just not up to it."

As Toni picked up the boy, the man in the crane set off the climactic display, a thirty-five-foot wheel of rockets so spectacular that it eclipsed all that had gone before. As it spun to a blazing climax, Toni watched the eager, excited face of the little boy she was holding in her arms. He was completely in awe of the whirling mass of blazing white rockets. In his innocence, he accepted the vision as magical, his enjoyment of it undiminished by an adult's awareness of the reality behind the illusion.

As the rocket spun to a finish, the child's full pink lips parted in a long, softly drawn out "ooh" of indescribable pleasure.

Watching him, Toni smiled wistfully, feeling a sense of loss, of regret, for the wonder and innocence that the child had and that she had lost.

Suddenly she was aware of someone watching them. Only a few feet away, a photographer stood focusing his camera on Toni and the boy. The man looked up just as Toni turned to see him, and their eyes met unexpectedly.

He was fairly tall, nearly six feet, Toni guessed. Though he was ruggedly built, there was something graceful about the sure manner in which his hands handled the intricate-looking camera slung around his neck on a worn leather strap. His black hair curled around the collar of his denim jacket and brushed his earlobes. The smooth, finely drawn planes and angles of his face seemed vaguely familiar to Toni, but she couldn't remember where she had seen him before.

What captivated her, however, were his eyes. They were a deep, dark chocolate brown. And they seemed to mirror in an uncanny way her own feelings at that moment. He, too, was clearly fascinated by the child, and also felt the loss of childhood's innocence.

That moment of shared feeling, of an unspoken but profound connection, was over in a matter of seconds. Feeling unaccountably embarrassed, Toni put down the child. Then she joined the rest of the crowd that was starting to move away now that the fireworks were over.

As Toni was trying to decide where she might have the best luck in finding a taxi, she was startled to feel a hand gently but firmly take hold of her arm. A resonant, very masculine voice with an ironic edge to it said, "I'm going to call that picture, 'Modern Madonna.' The way you were looking at that child was almost spiritual." Then he added casually, "Hope you don't mind being photographed."

His accent was American, which didn't surprise Toni. Though denim jackets and expensive Japanese cameras are universal, there was something about the man's attitude, the way his eyes met hers boldly, that was distinctly American.

"You might have asked for my permission," Toni said formally. She was irritated at the way the man was walking beside her as if he knew her. She didn't intend to be picked up. As the crowd pressed them closely together, she tried to think of a polite but firm way of telling him so.

"If I talked to you first, it would have ruined the shot," the photographer responded. Then he continued, "So, you're American, too. I thought so. We tend to be easily recognizable. By the way, there's a great pub nearby. We could have a drink, avoid the crush in the streets."

"Sorry," Toni answered quickly, deciding the direct approach was best. "I have to be up early in the morning."

They had passed through Albert Gate and were now on the sidewalk outside the park. Deciding to walk to her hotel, which was less than a mile away, Toni finished coolly, "Good night."

To her amazement, his hold on her arm tightened as she started to break away. She looked back at him angrily, prepared to be downright insulting if it was necessary. But her irate words were cut short by a devastating smile. It lit his dark eyes and softened his face. And it was wryly understanding.

"My name is Theo Chakiris. I'm a freelance photographer covering the wedding for *Vogue* magazine. If you're determined to be skeptical, I'll show you my press badge. Now that I've properly introduced myself, you can stop thinking of me as a strange man looking for a girl to seduce."

Toni felt chagrined. He'd caught her cynical attitude perfectly. She hadn't always been so ready to think the worst of men. Marriage to a man who was flagrantly unfaithful had destroyed whatever trust she'd once had.

Looking at this man carefully for a long moment, Toni began to feel reluctant to simply walk away from him forever. Finally, she said with a bit less chill in her tone, "I *do* have to get up early. I'm covering the wedding, too, for a Los Angeles television station. Sorry."

This time there was a note of genuine regret in her voice, though she still had no intention of going anywhere with him.

The crowd, which was pouring out of the park now, was jostling them.

"We're holding up traffic," Toni continued. "I'd better be going. Good night."

But as she headed off across busy Knightsbridge, he dropped into place beside her.

"I'll walk you to your hotel," he insisted.

She surprised herself by not arguing.

Toni and Theo turned right onto Wilton Place, heading toward fashionable Belgravia. The street was quiet and dark this late at night. Only a few windows in the monumental white stucco mansions were lit. They passed small, charming squares, neither speaking as they walked side by side. The crowd quickly dispersed and soon there were only a few other people on the street.

As Toni walked quickly beside Theo, her head barely even with his shoulders, she could detect the faint aroma of his aftershave: subtle, frankly masculine, like the man himself. She liked it. He was refreshingly simple and straightforward compared to the men she knew in Los Angeles. Too many of them went in for gold chains and shirts unbuttoned down to unbecoming paunches; or designer jeans and cowboy boots that had never touched a stirrup.

Toni glanced at Theo, surreptitiously taking in his attire. The denim jacket was a perfect fit on his broad shoulders. A pale blue shirt was open just enough to reveal black hair curling thickly on his dark chest. His jeans were well worn but they looked nice on his slim hips and long legs. Everything about him was casual yet becoming. She'd bet pretentiousness wouldn't be his style.

To her chagrin, he caught her watching him. That engaging smile flashed once more as he said, "You're still trying to make up your mind about me, aren't you?"

Really, Toni decided uncomfortably, the man was like a cat. It was impossible to catch him unaware.

"Then tell me about yourself," she demanded irritably.

"No, it's *my* turn," he answered evenly. "You already know that I take pictures for a living, which is about all there is to know about me. I don't even know your name."

"Antonia Lawrence," she said reluctantly.

"But everyone calls you Toni, right?" he responded, once more adroitly getting past her attempts at being formal. He added unexpectedly, "You don't look like a television reporter."

"Why not?"

"They're usually tall and leggy. From what I can see, you do have terrific legs," he commented, looking down at her form-fitting white linen skirt that was slit up one side. "But you're too short."

"I handle it by cutting everyone else down to size," Toni responded curtly. Comments about her size always brought out her temper.

Theo laughed deeply. Then, with his dark eyes boldly raking over all five feet, two inches of her, he said, "I'll bet you do."

Toni felt herself blush, not so much at his words as his frankly appreciative appraisal of her.

"Are you married?" Theo asked suddenly.

"You don't see a ring, do you?" Toni answered.

"That doesn't necessarily answer my question."

"Yes, it does," Toni said pointedly.

She shivered, then pulled her thin lavender cashmere sweater more tightly around the matching silk blouse. Even in the middle of a particularly warm summer, London was much cooler at night than she was used to. In an instant, Theo had taken off his jacket and slipped it over her gently sloping shoulders.

"Oh, no," Toni began.

Her protest was cut off by his polite but firm, "I insist."

Toni reached up to pull the jacket around her. It still had the warmth of Theo's body and his smell, a mingling of aftershave and other aromas that was very nice.

They continued walking in silence for a while, passing Belgrave Square with its beautiful sunken garden. Following Upper Belgrave Street past the square, they eventually turned onto Eaton, heading toward Eaton Place.

The street was nearly deserted now. Walking beside Theo, in the darkness and quiet, Toni felt a growing intimacy with him. It was as if they were suddenly the only two people in all of London. The night that had begun so gaily with fireworks had quieted. Yet, in a way, Toni felt more excitement at this moment than she had earlier at the fireworks spectacle with its circus atmosphere.

"Where are you staying?" Theo asked, breaking the tense silence.

"At the Hotel Ninety-Nine, at 99 Eaton Place," Toni answered. Pointing down the street to a small but brightly lit sign, she explained, "It's just down there."

"I know the place. Small but classy."

Once more they were silent. The playful banter with its undertone of sexual attraction had subsided to something a bit less glib.

As they arrived at the steps of the hotel, Toni stopped and said awkwardly, "Well, thanks for walking me 'home,' so to speak. I'll look for your pictures in *Vogue*."

Handing Theo his jacket, she started into the hotel.

"Wait a minute," Theo said, stopping her. He looked at her determinedly. "You can't let it end here. We have a lot more to say to each other."

"Such as?" Toni couldn't resist asking.

"Such as, what are your politics, what do you like to eat, did you have a happy childhood, what movies do you like?" Grinning, he finished, "Everything except your sign."

Toni grinned, too, in spite of herself. "I'm relieved you don't want to know my sign. But as for the rest of it . . ." She hesitated, then finished softly, "Why don't we just let it end here. It's been pleasant. In a way, it's nice not really knowing too much about each other. We can keep our illusions."

"You're afraid," he said flatly.

"No," Toni insisted, stiffening proudly to her full height, which still left Theo towering over her. "I just want to avoid complications."

"You're *afraid*," Theo pressed, leaning toward her, his brown eyes looking down at her relentlessly.

"I am not!" she said angrily, immediately regretting the silly words that sounded like a petulant child's.

"Then *prove* it. Go out with me tomorrow night. The wedding will be over. You can't use that as an excuse to avoid me."

Frowning, Toni answered, "We might very well end up hating each other. What if you can't bear Republicans and I turn out to be a dyed-in-the-wool capitalist? Or what if you're a health food nut and I thrive on Twinkies?"

"That isn't what you're afraid of." His eyes were watching her shrewdly, and she felt distinctly uncomfortable.

"You don't even know me. Why on earth are you so interested in seeing me again?" Toni asked, trying to regain the offensive in their verbal sparring.

To her surprise, he answered seriously, his grin gone, "We shared something back in the park earlier. A moment when we both felt the same thing. It wasn't superficial. It was real. And it meant something."

Toni felt herself withdraw, both physically and emotionally, as she stepped back from him. She tried to close off her mind to the feelings that were flooding it. When Theo first appeared, she was simply afraid that he would make a pass. That would have been awkward because she had no intention of going to bed with someone she didn't know. Now, her fear went deeper, because he had brought up a possibility that was infinitely more dangerous. The possibility that it might be more than a one-night stand.

And he was right, of course, she had to admit to herself. She *had* felt something profound between them in that brief, electric moment in the park. It was especially unnerving because she had grown used to Robert's ice-cold lack of empathy.

To Toni's dismay, Theo wouldn't let her run away,

even figuratively. He continued on a lighter note as his finger softly brushed the underside of her chin, "Besides, you have the most gorgeous eyes I've ever seen. I'd like to see what they look like when they're not angry."

Unhappily, Toni felt another blush coming on. She hadn't blushed in years, even when Robert's trendy Hollywood friends were at their most flagrantly sexual. Now this persistent, irritating man had caused her to blush twice in one short evening. What's the matter, she asked herself bitterly, losing that famous Beverly Hills cool?

It was the touch of his hand that did it. When he took her arm earlier she couldn't feel much because of her blouse and sweater. But the feel of his hand, rough yet gentle, stroking her chin, skin against skin, was unnerving. He was a magnetic man and she suspected that he was aware just how magnetic he was.

"All right, but you don't know what you're getting into," Toni relented angrily, no longer feeling up to sparring with him.

"Do you know London very well?" he asked unexpectedly.

"No," she admitted, glad the conversation was taking a less personal turn.

"I do. And I'll show it to you tomorrow night."

"All of it?" Toni asked facetiously, her composure once more intact.

"No. Just the romantic parts," he answered, unnerving her once more.

As Toni passed through the doors of the hotel, Theo called after her, "Right here, eight o'clock." Before the doors closed behind her, she heard his cheerful, "Good night."

Taking her key from the yawning desk clerk, Toni pushed the button for the elevator. What a way to go out on a date, she thought, shaking her head; on a *dare*, of all things. As she entered the elevator and punched the button for her floor, she assured herself that he probably wouldn't show up. Which would be a tremendous relief, she insisted.

A tiny voice inside her asked, But what if he *does* come?

That, Toni knew, would be interesting.

# 2

~~~~~~~~~~

The dull rumble that is the special noise of London was even greater on the day of the royal wedding. From Pall Mall to Ludgate Hill, London was awash with people waving Union Jacks. From a special vantage point near St. Paul's Cathedral, Toni covered the entire event, from the moment when a stately procession of horse-drawn carriages bearing the royal family left Buckingham Palace, to the shouts of "We love you!" from the crowd as the newlyweds rode off in an open landau ahead of the queen.

Later, Toni moved to another vantage point near the palace, where she described Charles and Diana kissing on the balcony. When the Prince and Princess of Wales donned their traveling attire and took off in another open carriage for Waterloo Station and a train ride to their honeymoon destination, Toni summed up her feelings about this day.

"Life, which is often drab, was colorful and magnificent today. There was clockwork precision and storybook splendor; magic in the daylight and sentimentality and spectacle. The royal wedding offered the timeless appeal of a fairy tale—a dashing Prince Charming matched with the lovely daughter of an earl. The archbishop in medieval costume and the fanfares of trumpeters all belong to a lost age that will never come again."

Smiling into the camera, holding a microphone, Toni continued smoothly, "Diana was a radiant bride wreathed in ivory tulle and trailing a twenty-five-foot silken train. Charles was a romantic groom in full-dress naval uniform with medals and sword. They exchanged secretive smiles as the archbishop asked them to 'remain faithful to each other and live together in love until their lives end.' All of it was magnificently staged, but it was more than simply good theater. Because it was the marriage of special people, it glorified the institution of marriage, proclaimed the worth of the sacrament and made everyone's marriage take on a new luster. Somewhere at the center of all this display of extravagance lies a touching truth—a universal fact of human instinct—the need to share one's life with someone."

As Toni signed off with, "This has been Antonia Lawrence covering the royal wedding in London," there were tears in her eyes.

"You were fantastic!" Carol grinned, hugging her happily.

Though Toni was almost giddy with relief that she'd handled this pressure-filled assignment well, her mind wasn't entirely on Charles and Diana. It was on a Greek-American photographer with a heart-turning smile.

At eight o'clock that evening, as Prince Charles and his bride were beginning their honeymoon, Toni sat reading in her hotel room. Actually, she was doing a poor job of pretending to read. The book, a history of British royalty, had been open to the same page for half an hour. Every time Toni tried to take in the words printed on it, her mind wandered off on a thousand tangents, all of them having to do with Theo Chakiris. Would he like her attire, a thin wool crepe peasant blouse embroidered and sequined with Matisse-inspired designs, and a full, calflength skirt in sapphire velvet? . . . Where would he take her? . . . Would they continue their argumentative but admittedly stimulating banter, or would an awkward silence plague them? . . . Would he even come at all?

Suddenly Toni realized that the toe of her stiletto-heeled calfskin shoe was tapping impatiently against the carpet, while her fingers played with a tiny seed-pearl button on her blouse. This is ridiculous, she thought. I'm as nervous as I was on my first date.

In some ways, she had to admit, it was like her first date. She hadn't gone out with anyone since her divorce two years earlier. It had been well over seven years since she had a typical date, and she was dismayed now to realize how out of practice she felt. She talked comfortably, confidently with men every day in her work. Yet when she talked briefly with Theo, she felt inept.

She tried to persuade herself that her turbulent emotions about this man simply came from a natural awkwardness at getting back into the swim of things. He was attractive, but she was used to meeting attractive men. When she saw him again, *if* she saw him, she would feel nothing toward him. The attraction she remembered feeling last night was exaggerated, a product of overwork and, she admitted reluctantly, loneliness. He was just another guy, a bit more glib than most. . . .

When the knock came, she jumped, startled. And when she opened the door a moment later to find Theo standing there, with that familiar sardonic grin on his face, she was surprised. She really hadn't expected him to come. She was surprised, too, at the way he looked. Toni's highly critical mind had lessened him by degrees until, in her memory, he wasn't terribly attractive.

The truth was that in the bright light of her room, Theo was even more attractive than Toni had thought earlier.

His features were strong yet finely chiseled—a straight, narrow nose, angular jaw and dark eyes that were deep and compelling. His casual clothes of the night before hadn't done justice to his build. Tonight he was wearing a light, russet-colored turtleneck sweater and matching slacks, with a darker gabardine blazer.

For a moment Toni wondered what those broad shoulders would look like bare, how the sinewy thighs would feel . . .

Forcing herself to sound casual, she said, "Hi." Then, glancing at her watch, she finished, "Right on time."

"Did you expect me to be late?" he asked. Before she could answer, he added, "Or didn't you expect me at all?"

This won't do, Toni thought. I can't let him catch me off guard right off the bat. He was leaning against the door frame, one hand resting in a pocket, the other hanging loosely at his side. He seemed in no hurry to leave.

Grabbing a cream-colored wool shawl, Toni walked right up to him, pulling the door closed behind her. She assumed he would be forced to move, but to her annoyance he hesitated as she stood only a hairbreadth from him.

"You look terrific," he said, his eyes roving frankly over her and lingering for a long moment on the swell of her breasts visible at the top of the low-cut blouse. "The gypsy look suits you. I can just see you dancing around a campfire." Glancing down at her shoes, he finished firmly, "But those won't do. We're going to be walking a lot tonight."

"Walking?"

His smile deepened. "Obviously you don't know London very well. It was made for walking, not driving. Unless you're in a hurry—and we're not. We have all night."

"Not *all* night," Toni insisted pointedly.

He raised one black eyebrow quizzically and responded, "We'll see."

Without saying anything, Toni quickly slipped out of the tall heels and into some comfortable shoes.

"Let's go then," she said breezily, pushing past him as she did when she was on assignment and making her way through a horde of fellow reporters.

Downstairs, she found he had a cab waiting. "Just for the first leg of the trip," he explained, opening the door for her politely and extending a hand to help her in.

Toni felt more than a bit embarrassed because she had assumed earlier he wanted to stay in her room. Not wanting to dwell on the fact that she had misjudged him, she tried to make conversation.

"Where are we going?"

"A little place in Chelsea. Do you like Indian food? East Indian, that is."

"I don't know," Toni admitted reluctantly. It bothered her to realize that he had the upper hand. He knew the city and she didn't. He had even chosen a restaurant serving one of the few types of food she'd never tried. It was an uncomfortable reminder of Robert, who had always made it abundantly clear that he was the teacher and she the pupil. She'd never been on an equal footing with her illustrious husband, and now the evening with this stranger, as Toni persisted in thinking of him, was starting out the same way.

Her anger must have shown, for Theo asked, showing his first glimmer of doubt, "Would you rather try something else? Somehow, I thought you'd be more adventurous."

"Oh, no," Toni said quickly. She didn't know how to explain her reluctance without going into a discussion of her marriage, and she had no intention of doing that.

She finished, smiling slightly, "No, that sounds fine. Actually, I *am* pretty adventurous when it comes to food.

My grandmother taught me to be open minded about it. She had me eating *haute cuisine* when all my friends were still into peanut butter-and-jelly sandwiches."

"Do that again," Theo whispered.

"Do what?" Toni asked, confused.

"Smile. It changes your face completely, makes you look . . ." He hesitated for a moment, then finished softly, "Young and innocent."

"I suppose I look old and jaded, then?" Toni asked facetiously, trying to dispel the atmosphere of intimacy his one whispered word had created.

"No. Not jaded, just serious."

Toni didn't know what to say to this. She leaned back against the seat and watched London passing by them as the cab driver quickly maneuvered through the narrow streets. The sun was down, twilight had set in and soon it would be dark. Though the interior of the cab was large by American standards, Toni felt disturbingly close to Theo. When she moved her arm she felt the smooth material of his jacket. And she could smell his aftershave, that now familiar, pleasant, musky scent.

The way his brown eyes were watching her shrewdly was making her nervous. Trying once more to make small talk, she said, "I thought you were going to give me a guided tour of the city. Where are we now?"

Smiling that fleeting, devastating smile that made Toni catch her breath, he responded in a perfect imitation of a slightly bored tour guide. "We are now entering the pleasant residential section of Chelsea with many interesting old mansions and many more or less picturesque modern houses of red brick. It has been the residence of many eminent persons and to this day is the home of numerous artists. It prides itself on its artistic and bohemian atmosphere." Lapsing back into his own natural speech, he finished, "Actually, I chose it because it has one of the nicest stretches of walks along the Thames in the whole city. And since while walking there's nothing to

do but talk, I figured it would be a great way to get to
know you better. I have to be calculating about this
because you're obviously determined to keep up that
wall around you."

Stung, Toni replied, "That works both ways, you
know. I'll have the same opportunity of finding out all
about *you*."

She was gratified at the look of wariness that briefly
crossed his face. So, you've built walls, too, she thought.
You like to breach other people's defenses, but you don't
want your own attacked.

At that moment, the taxi stopped in front of the
Tandoori Restaurant on Fulham Road. When they entered, Toni was surprised to find it a small, unpretentious
place. Somehow she had expected Theo to try to impress
her with a more elegant dinner.

They were immediately seated at a table near a
window.

"Would you like a drink?" he asked as the turbaned
waiter handed them menus.

"Yes, white wine. Chablis, if they have it."

He ordered a bottle of French wine that Toni was
unfamiliar with. When the waiter had gone, he said, "Did
you ask for wine because you prefer it? Or because
you're afraid hard liquor will make you lose your inhibitions with me?"

Unable to resist, Toni responded slyly, "I suspect I'll
need all my faculties to keep up with you tonight."

Theo smiled, appreciating the rather backhanded compliment.

The waiter returned and after pouring the wine, took
their order for dinner. Toni had no idea what to order, but
she was determined not to ask Theo for advice. After
choosing something that sounded a bit more subdued
than the more spicey-sounding dishes, she leaned back in
the chair and sipped the wine. It was amazingly good,
cool and subtle, not too sweet or fruity. Theo had good

taste in wine, she had to admit. And clothes, she added, glancing briefly at his expertly tailored and obviously expensive jacket. And women? she wondered. His easy manner with her, in spite of her downright antagonism at times, showed he was comfortable with women. The confident way he handled her showed that he was experienced.

"Tell me about yourself," he urged, using the line that she was just about to spring on him.

"What exactly would you like to know?"

"Don't be so suspicious," he said unexpectedly. "This isn't the inquisition. I'm not asking for your deepest secrets, though I'm sure they're *very* interesting."

Toni began to play with her fork nervously. This wouldn't do. Somehow she would have to get off the defensive with this man.

She answered, all in one breath, "I was born and raised in Santa Barbara, graduated from Sarah Lawrence College with a degree in English Lit., got married and divorced and I work as a television reporter for a local L.A. station."

Leaning forward, her elbows on the table and her hands clasped in front of her, she finished, "Now, tell me about *you.*"

"Oh, no. I'm not through with you yet. That biography had some interesting holes in it. Were you a happy child, or miserable?"

"Very happy," Toni answered. "Except for a time after my parents were killed in a boating accident. I was five. But I was raised by my grandmother, who's marvelous," she concluded, glossing over the terror she'd felt when she lost the people who were at the center of her young world. She had no intention of delving into such intimate emotions with Theo. Only her closest friends knew the really personal things about her. With everyone else, she kept up the image of a confident, happy young woman. It was true enough, as far as it went.

"You must have been terrified," Theo said soberly.

Taken aback, Toni didn't know how to respond. Her firm restrictions on what she was willing to reveal about her personal life didn't seem to hold with this man. He wanted to know the truth, not the façade, and she found it difficult to deflect him.

"As I said, my grandmother is marvelous," Toni answered simply. "I was all right." She took a long sip of wine. She wanted to get off this tender subject and go back to their verbal sparring. But he clearly wasn't going to let her.

"And the marriage?" he asked bluntly.

"Failed," Toni said curtly, her tone harsher than she'd intended.

"What happened?" Theo pressed, leaning back in his chair and watching her interestedly.

One thing Toni had learned from her grandmother, who was shrewd, is that giving away part of the truth often satisfies people. It makes them think they've gotten the whole truth. She decided to use this ploy with Theo.

"My ex-husband is Robert Lawrence, the novelist," she explained. "We came from very different backgrounds and had different . . . values. He wanted me to be a typical Beverly Hills matron, and I wanted a career. Our house on Beverly Drive was huge, but somehow it wasn't big enough for two egos. So we're divorced."

Everything she said was true. What was also true, and what she was determined not to talk about, were the five years of being told by Robert that he had talent and she didn't; that her value lay only in supporting his work; that she had no right to expect fidelity from him because it was an old-fashioned and completely useless virtue.

"I really didn't fit into his milieu," Toni finished, hoping that would be an end to the subject.

"Why not? You're beautiful and you dress well." Theo threw out the compliments offhandedly. "I thought that, and money, were all that matter in Beverly Hills."

In spite of herself, Toni was immensely flattered by the compliments. "I like to wear jeans too much, I guess," she said, smiling.

"But everyone in Beverly Hills wears jeans."

"Yes, but they're French. I prefer plain old Levis, the older and more faded, the better."

He laughed, an extremely pleasant, attractive sound, then continued more seriously, "I can't see you with Robert Lawrence. He's a brilliant writer, but he looks like a flamingo."

Remembering Robert, who was tall and thin and hook-nosed, with a penchant for wearing pink shirts, Toni burst out laughing. The simile was perfect—he *did* look like a flamingo, skinny-legged and pretentious.

"My grandmother didn't care for him, either," she finally managed to say when she'd stopped laughing.

"Your smile is nice but your laughter is even nicer," Theo said, his voice a bit husky. He was studying her intently, the wry amusement gone now from his voice.

His habit of handing out compliments at unexpected moments, and with such sincerity, threw Toni.

Before she quite recovered, he continued more casually, "How did you end up with him, anyway?"

"I studied his books in college, of course, and was deeply impressed. When I met him at a party in L.A. and he later proposed, everyone told me how lucky I was. I believed them, I guess. A classic case of the idol having feet of clay."

"When did you realize the truth?" Theo asked.

Toni was tempted to answer, "On our wedding night," remembering Robert's insensitive lovemaking. Instead, she said, "Rather quickly, actually. But I stuck it out for a long time. I guess I was too proud to admit I'd made such a stupid mistake. It ended pretty abruptly. I was setting the table for a special dinner Robert was having to celebrate the publication of his new book. He had picked out the china himself, and it was unbelievably expensive.

I accidentally dropped a plate. Robert came in, shouting furiously, '*How* did that happen?' Well, something snapped. I said, 'Like this,' and dropped a whole armful of plates. I walked out and never looked back."

Theo laughed uproariously, and Toni found herself giggling with him as she remembered the marvelous sense of release she'd felt at that moment.

"I knew you couldn't possibly be as prim as you try to behave," Theo finally said, when he'd stopped laughing.

Fortunately, at that moment the waiter brought their dinner. Toni used the diversion to end the conversation about her marriage and her true character.

"Ooh," Toni breathed, as she took a bite of the curry. Quickly, she grabbed the wine glass and downed a good bit of it. The dish was delicious, but quite hot.

"I would have warned you about that," Theo said, smiling, "but you clearly prefer to find your own way."

Toni had the good grace to look embarrassed. He was right. After her experiences with Robert, she had a chip on her shoulder when it came to being told what to do. She wouldn't have listened to Theo's advice.

He asked the waiter to bring Toni a tall glass of water, and she continued eating. But she alternated the food with generous amounts of wine and water.

They had just finished their dinner and were waiting for the waiter to bring coffee, when a man stopped by the table. He was tall and heavyset, with a thick brown beard and shaggy brown hair.

"Theo, I should have known you'd be here," he said happily, in an accent that left no doubt he came from New York.

"It's good to see you, Charlie," Theo responded, clearly meaning it. Then, motioning to Toni, he said, "Toni Lawrence, I'd like you to meet Charlie Bickham. Charlie's a documentary film maker. Are you here for the wedding, too?" he asked, turning toward Charlie.

Pulling up a chair and joining them, Charlie said, "Hell,

no, I'm just passing through on my way back to New York from Lebanon. Been doing a film on the P.L.O. Don't tell me you're actually covering this soap opera?"

Theo laughed deprecatingly. "What can I say? I was in Northern Ireland working on a story when *Vogue* called and offered me an obscene amount of money to do this. Apparently the guy they lined up got sick at the last minute."

"That's more like it. Your pictures usually have guns and grenades in them, not brides and grooms."

"Well, I'll be back in Northern Ireland tomorrow," Theo replied. "There are plenty of guns and grenades there."

Toni looked up quickly from the coffee she was sipping. Theo hadn't mentioned to her that he was leaving the next day. Well, so what? she asked herself soberly. You're leaving tomorrow, too. So that makes it easier all around.

Still, a tiny pinprick of surprise and disappointment remained.

"Are you here for the wedding, Toni?" Charlie asked, turning toward her.

"Yes," she answered. "I work for an L.A. television station."

"L.A., huh? This stuff should go over big there. It's just like a movie anyway."

Toni smiled. "I take it you don't find it romantic and fascinating?"

"Oh, I don't object to it. The British handle pageantry better than anyone, though it's about all they do right nowadays."

"Well, Charlie," Theo interrupted what was promising to become an extended conversation between Toni and Charlie. "I'd like to invite you to join us but I'm sure you're *very* busy."

Charlie laughed. "I get it. Three's a crowd." Shooting a quick, appreciative glance at Toni, he added, "I don't blame you, Theo." Rising, he continued, "Give me a call before you leave. I'm at the Dorchester." Then, taking Toni's hand and squeezing it gently, he finished, "Nice to meet you. If you find yourself in New York, Toni, give me a call."

And then he was gone.

Eyeing Theo carefully, Toni said wryly, "You were rude."

"Of course. It was the only way to get rid of him. In case your modesty won't let you see it, he was coming on to you." Theo continued, more seriously, "Charlie's my oldest friend. It's impossible for us to insult each other."

"How did you meet?" Toni asked, determined to use this opening to find out more about Theo. He knew so much about her, much more than she had intended to reveal, while she knew nothing about him.

"We generally wind up in the same places. We both specialize in covering wars. The first one was Viet Nam. Since then, we've been all over the world together. El Salvador, the Middle East, South Africa. More places than I can remember. War is always popular, you know," he finished, a cynical note to his voice now.

His dark eyes had turned thoughtful and introspective, but also guarded. He looked away, taking a long sip of coffee.

So this is where your wall starts, Toni thought wonderingly.

"Why do you do that?" she asked frankly. "Cover wars, I mean."

"Someone has to," he answered defensively. Then, with a bitter-edged humor, "It's a dirty job but someone's got to do it."

"Why?" Toni persisted.

He rested one forearm on the edge of the table and leaned forward slightly. "I didn't grow up wanting to photograph death and destruction. I went to Nam because so many guys I knew were fighting there. I was curious about it. I stayed with the soldiers, ate like them, lived like them. After awhile, I began to feel akin to them. I saw men, boys really, killed and no one seemed to care. I took pictures of it so people *would* care, so they would *never* forget."

"*You* cared, didn't you." It was a statement, not a question.

Theo tried for a tone of indifference. "Hell, I know that a few pictures aren't going to stop wars."

Toni let it ride. She would have liked to know more about him, especially *his* deepest secrets. But she wasn't prepared to trade her own in exchange.

"Where do you come from?" she asked on a lighter note.

"San Francisco," Theo answered quickly, clearly relieved that the conversation was taking a less probing turn. "My father emigrated from Greece in the thirties and settled there. He was a fisherman, as hardnosed as they come." Theo fingered his water glass nervously. Toni realized that here were deep waters, also. Quickly changing the subject, Theo finished, "My two older brothers still live there. They own a restaurant together."

When Theo mentioned that his father was Greek, Toni suddenly realized why she had thought he looked familiar when she first met him. He reminded her of Greek statues she had seen in museums, with their timeless idealization of male beauty. Theo had that same quality of being physically perfect without seeming at all effeminate.

Dwelling on Theo's considerable physical attractions made Toni flush nervously. She hurried to take her mind off this disturbing line of thought. "Do you get back to San Francisco often?"

"Every once in a while." Then he continued drily, "I'm the black sheep of the family. My brothers did the normal things, establishing a business, getting married, having lots of curly-haired kids. Here I am running around the world taking pictures, most of which aren't very pleasant. They think it isn't the right thing for a grown man to be doing."

"But it's what you've always wanted to do," Toni said in a flash of insight.

"Yeah," Theo responded, surprised at her perception. Then he finished lightly, "And here I am taking pictures of the marriage of an unemployed man and a girl whose primary virtue seems to be the fact that she's a virgin."

Irritated, Toni responded, "Is *that* how you see this?"

"That's how it *is*," he answered. "What does the royal family do? Open institutions, preside at banquets, visit the theater."

"I think there's a great deal more than that to this wedding. You'd see it if you'd stop being cynical for a moment."

"What do *you* think this media circus has?" Theo asked.

"Well, on a superficial level, it gives so many people a great deal of enjoyment. It *is* a beautiful spectacle. And on a deeper level, it is an affirmation of marriage, commitment, love, whatever you want to call it," she finished quickly, suddenly embarrassed.

"Is that how you see it?"

"I think it's a terrific story to cover," Toni said evasively. Then, more firmly, "Think what you like. But from what I could see, Charles and Diana really love each other. And that's a nice change from the way relationships normally go nowadays. When the archbishop asked them if they would 'remain faithful to each other and live together in love until their lives end,' it was"— she paused, searching for the right word—"well, a lovely thought."

"It *does* have a nice ring to it," Theo admitted. Then he continued drily, "But in a world of premarital contracts, palimony, galimony, and the rest of it, I think it's unrealistic to talk about loving forever."

"*You* are a cynic," Toni said flatly.

"And *you* are a romantic," Theo responded, smiling. "Of the two of us, you're going to get shot down more often than I will."

"Perhaps, but I'll survive," Toni shot back defiantly.

Theo laughed, a deep, rich sound. "Do you *ever* give up?"

"Sometimes," Toni answered softly, thinking of her marriage.

Theo looked up at her sharply, in obvious understanding. Before he could say anything, Toni finished hurriedly, "I thought you were going to show me London. So far, all I've seen is some incredibly spicy food."

"Come on," he said, rising and pulling back her chair. He tossed some pound notes on the table, then helped her slip into her shawl. His hands rested on her shoulders for just a moment longer than was necessary. Though Toni's back was turned to him, she felt his presence powerfully. Her hair brushed his chest and her hands trembled as she tied the shawl into a loose knot.

Outside, the night was cool and dark. Toni was glad she'd remembered to bring a warm wrap.

They walked for a long way, in silence, before reaching the river. The Thames was broad and dark and flowed gently. The water flickered in the moonlight.

"This is called the Chelsea Embankment," Theo explained, his voice sounding oddly tense in the silence. "It's about a mile from here to Battersea Bridge. I thought we'd walk down there, then turn back toward the city."

"Okay," Toni nodded.

They proceeded, once more in a companionable silence, past narrow gardens and rows of red brick Georgian houses behind wrought-iron railings. It was a lovely, picturesque area, and Toni wished she had time to visit it in the daytime. As they walked along in the cool, quiet darkness, hearing the gentle lap of the water against the embankment, Toni found herself thinking about Theo's cynical words about the wedding. "Do you *really* think this wedding is such a farce?" she asked, turning to look up at him.

"Of course. It was a fable. When the fable ends, reality intrudes."

"For this couple, though, the enchantment of once upon a time is supposed to last and last," Toni said softly.

"I don't think it lasts for anyone," Theo replied firmly.

"I'll bet your hero is Scrooge," Toni said bitingly. "You probably say 'bah, humbug,' to anything that even remotely smacks of romance."

"I'm not against romance. I'm just realistic about it. All good things come to an end, as they say."

"Were you ever married?" Toni asked abruptly. She had been wanting to ask the question all evening, but was reluctant to show too great an interest in Theo's love life. Now, however, she threw caution to the wind.

"No. I travel around too much. I've never been in one place for longer than a couple of months since I started working as a photographer."

"Which means your life is a series of one-night stands, with perhaps a short-lived affair thrown in here and there," Toni said tersely. She knew it was a rotten, judgmental thing to say. And she certainly had no right to criticize his lifestyle. Besides, there was no reason why she should care what he did with his life, she reminded herself.

"Right," Theo responded angrily. "And if we're going to get personal, I'd like to know about your sex life. Or was marriage to an idiot like Lawrence enough to make you celibate?"

Though Toni realized deep inside she had asked for the

painful, far-too-personal attack, she was too angry to be reasonable or fair. She whirled around, her back to the river, facing Theo squarely, forcing him to stop abruptly. She looked like a kitten standing up to a bulldog. Her eyes were blazing and her chin was held just a bit too high, as if she were daring Theo to take a punch at her.

Theo's expression was one of barely controlled anger, but far from being intimidated by him, Toni felt compelled to run straight into that anger. All evening she had felt a growing sense of something smoldering between them. She tried desperately now to bank that blazing fire by turning it into a bitter argument that would leave them both hating each other.

"Does it bruise your fragile male ego to think I might choose to have nothing to do with men? To think I don't need or want any of you?" Her nerves came alive, her pulse was racing, as she stood only inches from him.

For one moment, the world itself seemed to stop spinning, the muted night noises around them seemed to be silenced. It was as if time itself had stopped.

Theo looked furious, and in his fury there was a hardness that came down over his face like a mask. The sardonic grin was gone. The features that were so appealing when they were relaxed seemed harsh now. Toni half expected him to hit her. At the very least, she expected a verbal lashing.

As they both stood trembling on the brink of a precipice neither could avoid, something in Theo snapped. The anger drained from his face, to be replaced by an even more elemental instinct. Pulling Toni to him roughly, oblivious at the moment to whether or not he might hurt her, he pinned her against him. Then he kissed her deeply, with an urgency that overwhelmed Toni.

Feeling the lean hardness of Theo's body, Toni was inflamed by a surge of passion so compelling that it filled the emptiness within her. The aching yearning she had felt for so long was gone now, as Theo crushed her lips beneath his own demanding ones.

Eventually Theo pulled back, leaving Toni with a drugging warmth, her body languid now instead of rigid. His brown eyes looked at her, searching, questioning. Instead of reflecting the arrogance of victory, they were thoughtful, almost shy. She knew he had intended to put her in her place. Instead, she could tell that he himself was profoundly shaken by their kiss.

His voice, when he finally spoke, was a husky caress. "Toni. . . ."

Her breath came raggedly, and Toni couldn't respond.

Silently, Theo put an arm around her shoulder with infinite tenderness, and together they walked away from the river.

For a long while, neither said anything, as they passed under huge, spreading chestnut trees. Only a few stars shone through the cloudy night, and the moon was a hazy, dim glow in the far distance. It was dark, peaceful, quiet. Toni was still adjusting to the fact that her defenses had been breached in a way she wasn't prepared for. She sensed that Theo felt the same. The spark that had been ignited between them the very moment their eyes first met could no longer be contained.

Toni knew instinctively what would happen now. Yet, like a child reveling in the tantalizing pain of waiting on the night before Christmas, she wanted to savor these new feelings before exploring them fully. She was filled with a trembling eagerness.

Toni's tousled, coppery curls lay gently on Theo's shoulder. The gabardine jacket was cool and smooth. His arm was gently protective around her, as they walked slowly, quietly. She almost thought she could hear the beating of his heart.

They were nearly at Green Park when they saw an old-fashioned open carriage approaching. The horse was trotting along smartly, his hooves clicking on the paved road. The driver wore a tall, dark top hat and cutaway coat.

Motioning to the driver, Theo stopped, waiting as the carriage pulled beside them. "Are you available?" he asked.

"I *was* on my way 'ome," the man answered in a thick cockney accent. Then, taking a long look at Theo and Toni standing closely together, he smiled and said, "But I can use one more fare. 'Op in, Sir, Ma'am."

Theo gave the driver the address of Toni's hotel, then settled them both comfortably in the leather-covered seat. They were silent once more as the carriage took them quickly through the streets that were busier, more noisy now. The quiet, quaint charm of Chelsea and the darkly flowing Thames were far behind them as they headed into the center of the city.

As they passed Hyde Park, Theo said suddenly, "Would you mind taking us for a turn through the park?"

"'Course not, guv'nor," the driver answered, heading the horse into the quiet, empty park. "Young love," he whispered, in a barely audible voice, shaking his head slightly.

As they drove through the vast park, Toni realized with a jolt that it had only been the night before that she had met Theo here. Twenty-four hours. In that short time, she had gone from a profound emptiness to an awareness of what she had been missing during her marriage. Sleeping Beauty brought back from her deep slumber couldn't have felt a deeper sense of awakening. Until that moment by the river, Toni had never fully realized the intense, compelling bond that can exist between a man and a woman. Robert had touched every inch of her body without making her feel anything. With one kiss, Theo made her feel almost everything there was to be felt. And more remained, she knew.

The driver stopped at the hotel, grinning broadly as

Theo tipped him generously. Then he whipped the horse briskly into a trot and quickly disappeared.

Until they reached the door of her room, neither Toni nor Theo said anything. As she opened the door, then turned to face him, he seemed uncharacteristically hesitant. Toni realized that it was up to her now. Theo wouldn't force her.

"I'd like you to come in," she said, her voice whispery soft. She wanted this man who thrilled her, who had probably known a hundred women. Whatever the past had been, whatever the future might be, she wanted this night with him. He had tantalized her with a glimpse of what could be between a man and a woman. She wanted to know it all. She had waited too long for that knowledge.

As he closed the door behind them, Theo said tentatively, "Toni, I . . ."

"No, don't say anything," she answered. Then, a slow, shy smile spreading across her face, she finished, "I think the time for talk is past."

His dark eyes were lit by a secret amusement then. His firm mouth relaxed almost imperceptibly into a slight smile. He walked up to her, taking her hands in his and wrapping them softly around his neck. She had to stand on tiptoe, and after a moment, he simply pulled her up bodily until her face was level with his. He kissed her deeply, as he had before, but with an even greater demand. His passion was undiminished now by anger, as he pulled her against him. She responded fully, her inhibitions gone, feeling no fear or nervousness, only a breathless joy.

He carried her to the bed, then lay down beside her, propping himself up on one elbow to look down at her adoringly. As she ran her fingers through his thick, dark hair, then ran them lightly along the nape of his neck, he groaned softly with pleasure. While his mouth sought

hers once more, he held her against him, molding her
body to his. They were locked together tightly now. The
relentlessly growing desire in each had reached a point of
no return.

His breathing became shallow as he looked down at
her once more, his dark eyes smoldering with passion.
She looked back at him, not trusting herself to speak,
hoping her eyes told him how much she wanted him. She
was dazed with the intensity of her desire for him.

But she sensed that he wanted to go slowly with her
now, to control, for the moment, his demanding virility.
His tenderness and consideration revealed that he was
more concerned with her pleasure than his own. This
touched her deeply. Something in his passionate yet
gentle gaze told her that he knew that in the fullest sense
she was still innocent and untouched.

Toni wanted desperately to feel all the sensations she
had never felt before. And she was sure that this man,
who obviously knew women well, could take her to that
special place.

In a movement that was remarkably smooth and deft,
Theo slipped off her blouse and skirt. Now, she was
wearing only a China silk camisole and ruffled petticoat
trimmed with ribbons and lace. Slowly, with agonizing
deliberateness, he undid each of the tiny buttons that ran
down the front of the camisole. Toni wore no bra
underneath, and as he got to the last button, he caught a
glimpse of the valley between her breasts. Glancing at
her to make sure that there was no fear in her eyes,
he was clearly relieved to see only a shy but eager curiosity.

He carefully removed the camisole, leaving her half
exposed. Her breasts were small but full and round,
perfectly shaped and firm. Before he even touched them,
the nipples were pink and erect. He traced the gentle
swell of her breasts with a touch as light as a feather.

Every nerve in her body came alive.

"You are so beautiful," he whispered, his voice raw.

"Theo," she breathed softly, feeling herself blush once more at his frank, admiring glance. Then, before control left her entirely, she hurried to explain, "I'm not really very experienced . . ."

"Shh," he whispered, putting one finger to her trembling lips. She barely felt the gentle touch, yet it inflamed her. "I'll give you all the experience you need."

His hands moved with tantalizing purposefulness along the sides of her body, quickly removing the petticoat. As she lay there naked and proud under his probing gaze, he drew her tightly to him, running one hand along her back, from the nape of her neck, past her slim waist to her gently rounded hips. Unconsciously, she pressed her body against him, reveling in the sensuous feel of his smooth jacket and soft shirt against her bare skin.

She began to tremble slightly. To calm her, Theo caressed her face, then kissed her eyelids, cheeks and chin. His mouth traveled slowly down to her neck and then to the soft rise of her breasts.

He continued to explore her body with an exquisite tenderness that had her catching her breath. As he came to know her intimately, she was relieved to see a fierce desire in his eyes. He wanted her as much as she wanted him, she knew, but he was taking the time to be gentle and patient out of concern for her.

Rising up on one arm, he started to unbutton his shirt. His chest was broad and dark, covered with short, curly tendrils that looked coarse but were surprisingly soft to her tentative touch. As she began to explore his body with a frank desire that overcame her awkward embarrassment, she sensed that the last remnants of his control were slipping away. It was unbearably sensuous for her, feeling the dawning of profound desire.

Quickly shedding the remainder of his clothes, he reached over to the bedside lamp and turned out the light. The quick glimpse she got of his body before the light was extinguished was enough to dispel any lingering hesitation on her part. The only man she had ever slept with was Robert. She was used to his thin, unappealing body; his urgent, selfish lovemaking. Theo was so different. His body was ruggedly masculine and well-muscled, his shoulders broad and firm, his thighs sinewy and powerful.

His lovemaking was provocatively tender yet passionate. In response, her hands were exploring him unashamedly now, with clear delight.

He took the time to arouse her to his own fever pitch before taking her demandingly in his powerful arms, skin against skin along the full length of their impassioned bodies. By the dim light of the hazy moonlight filtering through the window, Toni gave herself as she had never done before. Fulfilled by Theo's expert lovemaking, she was consumed by a raging inferno. When her eyes met his briefly, she saw that he, too, was burning with desire. And when the two fires met, they consumed the hunger that fed their fury. . . .

Sometime in the early hours of the morning, before the sun had risen, Theo rose and dressed quietly. Toni watched him silently. There were a million things she longed to say, but not one she was willing to voice.

As Theo slipped on his jacket, he turned to glance at her in the dimness of the room.

"I'll call you," he said softly.

Toni shook her head firmly. "No. Let's just . . . let's just say good-bye."

Walking over to the bed, he bent down to peer closely at her. Pressing one finger to her lips gently, he insisted, "I'll call you."

As he opened the door, he turned and said softly,

"Toni, I . . ." Unwilling, or unable, to continue, he stopped, leaving the thought unexpressed.

And then he was gone, the door closing firmly behind him.

Toni turned over and buried her head in the pillow. It was a long time before she finally fell into a fitful, troubled sleep.

# 3

~~~~~~~~~~~~~~

The insistent ringing of the alarm clock cut through the fog of sleep, forcing Toni to wake up. Sitting up reluctantly and rubbing her eyes tiredly, Toni looked around at the room flooded with sunlight. Yawning, she rose and went into the bathroom to wash the sleep from her eyes.

Looking at herself in the mirror, she thought, It's really over. London is thousands of miles away, and so is Theo. It would be best to think of it all as just a lovely dream, something that wasn't real.

She realized now that it wasn't so much Theo who was important, as his effect on her. Their brief time together had taught her so much, had been so liberating. With him, she had discovered her womanhood in a way that she hadn't done with Robert. It frightened her to think she could feel so deeply about a man, but at the same time it was reassuring. There were times with Robert when she had wondered if *she* was at fault, if she was inadequate somehow; perhaps even frigid. That was a frightening word that she never used out loud, but it haunted her.

Theo had exorcized that ghost, at least. She knew now

how passionate she could be. What a shame, she thought, with her typical dry humor, there's no man around to reap the benefits. Actually, she had tried dating once since her return to L.A. An old college flame, someone she'd dated half seriously before marrying Robert, had come to town. He had been very attractive in college and was even more appealing now, with an experienced, worldly air that suited him. Yet when he kissed her at the end of the evening outside her front door, she didn't invite him inside.

Theodopolus Chakiris, you've spoiled me for anyone else, Toni told herself silently as she brushed her hair. Then, irritated with the fact that she couldn't get him out of her mind even when she slept, she said out loud, "I'm glad I'll never see him again!"

But her lovely violet eyes were infinitely sad and were filled with an intense longing.

# 4

~cccccccccc~

Theo looked down into Gayle Gerard's catlike green eyes. They were half closed, and the expression on her flawless face was sated. Though she was clearly satisfied by their lovemaking, there was no tenderness or affection in the way her heavy-lidded eyes gazed back at him lazily. Rolling over onto his side of the bed, Theo looked up at the ceiling. He couldn't understand why the hell he felt so incomplete. Gayle was terrific in bed, completely uninhibited. And her long-legged body had driven more than one man crazy with desire.

As she rose, drawing a silk robe loosely around her shoulders, she moved with a feline grace. Theo watched her objectively, strangely unmoved by the way she deliberately left the robe open at her voluptuous breasts. It was so typical of Gayle to try to arouse him again quickly.

"How long will you be in L.A.?" she asked, leaning down to kiss him lightly.

"I'm not sure. Maybe a long time," he responded absently.

"Well, sugar, unfortunately, I have to leave in two days. Too bad. You're really something, as you damn well

56

know. I wish I was going to be around to enjoy you a bit more."

Far from being flattered by Gayle's frank compliments, Theo was put off by them. Suddenly, he was glad she was leaving so quickly. After one evening with her, he was bored.

"I'll be back soon, though," she continued, sitting on the edge of the bed, brushing her long blonde hair. It was a stunning champagne color, yet somehow Theo found himself thinking of flaming-red curls.

"The network's after me to do a story on Hollywood," she explained, her face averted as she continued brushing her hair. Gayle was a network reporter who specialized in interviews involving famous people. She was ruthlessly ambitious and highly successful.

Until tonight, Theo had found her the perfect mistress —sexually liberated, completely uninterested in commitment. He continued staring at the ceiling, wondering why he'd felt so little pleasure with her this time.

"Why don't we have room service bring up some dinner," Gayle suggested. "No sense in wasting what little time we have going out."

Her green eyes watched him slyly as a devilish smile played around her full lips.

Suddenly, Theo knew that he wanted nothing more to do with her. "Sorry, babe, I've got to go."

He didn't bother with an explanation. And though Gayle was clearly surprised and disappointed, she didn't ask any questions. Their relationship didn't include either explanations or questions.

Later, back in his own hotel room, he stood looking out of the window, a glass of brandy in one hand. His other hand rested loosely in a pocket, while he stared out at the lights of L.A. Taking a sip of brandy, he felt it burn as it went down. But the jolt cleared his mind. For a month now, he'd been running away from something. His reaction to Gayle tonight had finally made it clear that running away wasn't working. He would have to stop and face what was bothering him.

You're slipping, old man, he told himself cynically, when you can't get violet eyes and glorious red hair off your mind.

Raising his glass in a silent toast, he thought, Here's to you, Antonia Lawrence. You've cast a spell over me that keeps you in my thoughts constantly. It's about time I found out if that spell can be broken.

The newsroom at station KABN was small, crowded and littered with a variety of typing paper, newspaper clippings and empty paper cups. The six o'clock news was just beginning, playing to the newsroom from a small portable television in a corner. In the glass-walled executive producer's office, a group of reporters and producers, including Carol, was gathered, watching the program.

Theo stood hesitantly in the doorway, looking for Toni. Finally, he saw her, standing at a desk at the far end of the room, putting away a tape recorder and note pad. Obviously, she was preparing to go home.

Theo's voice broke through the low background noise of the television. "Toni."

He saw her shoulders stiffen beneath the thin material of her blouse. She hesitated for a moment before turning to face him.

She looked surprisingly the same. He was struck once more by her unusual violet eyes, narrowed now in unwelcoming coolness.

She was wearing the white linen skirt she'd worn that first night in London, with a different, peach-colored silk blouse. In an uncanny way, it almost seemed as if there hadn't been a whole month between then and now.

She finished putting away her things and picked up her small leather shoulder bag. "Hello, Theo," she said casually, disinterestedly.

Lady, I admire your cool, he thought, amazed at how well she was hiding her shock at seeing him so unexpectedly.

He put one hand restlessly in a pocket, then took it out again. Suddenly, he was acutely ill at ease. And he could tell that Toni was determined to do nothing to alleviate that. "I remembered your mentioning where you work," he explained, then stopped, at a loss for what to say next. In his career as a war photographer, he'd been in dangerous places. Never had he felt as nervous as he did now.

"Oh? If you'd come earlier, I would have given you a tour of the place," she answered politely, as if she were talking to a new acquaintance. "But I'm just on my way out now. So, if you'll excuse me . . ."

She started to brush past him, but he placed one hand on her arm, stopping her. He had a flash of *déjà vu* as he remembered the first time he'd touched her in Hyde Park when she attempted to walk away from him.

"I deserve your rejection," he said soberly. "I should have called."

"I told you not to bother."

He didn't know what to say to that. Her temper, he could deal with. Even a carefully controlled politeness was a defense mechanism he could get around. But this indifference. . . .

Then, seeing how rigidly she held her shoulders, how she studiously avoided looking at him directly, he realized that she wasn't really indifferent.

"I said I would call you and I didn't do it. I don't blame you for being furious with me now."

"Forget it. Now, if you'll excuse me . . ."

"No, I *won't* forget it. I don't think you've forgotten it."

He was determined now, no longer awkward or hesitant. During the long weeks he'd thought about her, he'd envisioned many types of reunions. Generally his scenarios featured a furious Toni lashing out at him, at least verbally if not physically. He hadn't anticipated this icy calm. But it no longer threw him. He realized now that her pride was responsible. Her pride was greater than her temper. And while she was undoubtedly livid with him, she wouldn't let him see that.

She was such a small, pathetically proud figure that he wanted to take her in his arms right then. But he couldn't. He knew he would have to wait for the right time.

"We don't have anything to say to each other, Theo," Toni finished, brushing past him.

As she quickly walked out of the newsroom, he followed her. She was opening the door of her small, white Mercedes convertible when Theo spoke again.

"I think we have a lot to say to each other, Toni. In London we barely scratched the surface."

Toni winced at the casual mention of London.

Seeing her pained reaction, Theo continued more gently, "Have dinner with me. Please."

"No." There was no anger in her voice, only a quiet stubbornness.

"I expected that. And I deserve it, I guess. You're paying me back. But I'm not going to accept it."

"Oh? Do you have any choice?"

She turned her back on him as she got in the car. A moment later, she started the engine. He stood there, holding the door open, knowing that in a second she would pull the door closed and drive away. Forever. He had to do something *fast*. He'd been in enough tight situations before in his work, where he had to act fast. He did so now.

"You think all I wanted was a one-night stand, that once I got what I wanted, I didn't care about you." He was laying it out bluntly, brutally honest, knowing it would hurt her. But he also knew that straightforward honesty was the only way to get past her determined, unrelenting coolness.

It worked. He was relieved, yet sad, to see a hurt look

cross her face and dim those lovely eyes. But at least I've reached her, he thought, relieved.

"You have *no* idea what I think." Her voice wasn't quite so calm now. There was a brittle edge to it that revealed how close she was to tears.

But she was hesitating. The engine was still running quietly, but she was making no move to close the door.

He smiled briefly then. "I *know* what you must have been thinking," he responded, more at ease now. "Because it's what anyone would think. I told you I would call and I didn't. That was a month ago and I haven't contacted you since. It's only logical that you would assume I took what I could get then disappeared. I've gotta say, the way those gorgeous eyes are looking at me right now, I feel like a heel."

Toni apparently hadn't realized how hard she was staring at him, how intently she was listening to his words. Embarrassed, she looked away, fiddling with the keys dangling from the ignition. Abruptly, Theo reached over and turned off the motor. For one brief second, his face was only inches from hers, his arm brushing her breasts as he reached across her. Then he pulled back, leaving both of them momentarily shaken.

Toni answered drily, "So, if you're such an admitted heel why should I bother talking to you, let alone have dinner with you?"

"Because you look hungry, for one thing," Theo said, taking in the form-fitting blouse and linen skirt that were a bit too large for her. He guessed she'd lost about seven pounds. On her tiny frame, that was a great deal. But her figure was still surprisingly lush for such a small body. God, she's beautiful, Theo thought. Even more beautiful than I remembered.

"That's not enough," Toni replied. "Why didn't you call? If it *did* mean more to you than just a one-night stand, why did you disappear for a month?"

He knew she was purposefully being as blunt as he

was. If he had an excuse, she wanted to hear it. And it had better be a good one, he knew.

"Have dinner with me and I'll tell you the whole story."

"No. Tell me now."

"A parking lot isn't the right place. I would prefer someplace dark and intimate, with a romantic atmosphere that will help me get rid of that chip on your shoulder."

"If you need the right background, then your story must be pretty thin."

"No. But I *do* admit I want all the help I can get. Because I suspect you're not the sort of person who forgives easily."

"I don't think this is a great time to be criticizing *my* character, to be dissecting *my* shortcomings. If you're trying to put me on the defensive, it isn't working," Toni said flatly.

"Damn it, Toni!" Theo exploded. "Give me a chance!" He was angry at himself for handling this so badly, and angry at her for not making it any easier. She managed to get past his carefully maintained aura of cool cynicism more than anyone he'd ever known, and he didn't know how to deal with that. The woman excited him, angered him, disconcerted him and fascinated him. It was a combination he found irresistible.

Her own temper snapped then. She let it all out. "You're right about what I think, Theo. I think you were looking for an easy pickup in London. You found it, and *that's* the whole story. I don't know why on earth you're here now, unless you're passing through L.A. and looking for another one-night stand. Well, forget it."

"I'm sorry I got angry," Theo began.

Before he could finish, Toni responded, "Good-bye, Theo," and started to close the door.

"Isn't there anything I can say?" he shouted angrily.

"No!"

"Not even that I haven't been able to get you out of my mind since that night? I don't know how the hell to handle that because it's never happened before."

She hesitated with the door nearly shut. He saw that she hadn't expected that and didn't know how to react to it.

"That's a clever line," she finally managed to say softly.

"I don't know how clever it is, but it isn't a line. It's true. I didn't call you, I didn't get in touch with you all this time, because I was trying to forget about you. I tried damn hard. But I couldn't do it. You're right when you say that I was looking for a one-night stand in London. But that isn't what I found."

"What *did* you find?" she couldn't resist asking.

"I found someone I can't forget."

There was a long silence. Theo still stood beside the car, while Toni sat inside, her hand on the door handle. He knew that everything depended on this moment. There was nothing more he could say. If she still rejected him, it would be useless to pursue her any further.

Finally, Toni said softly, not looking at him, "Where do you want to go for dinner?"

Theo almost sighed with relief. It was all he could do to keep from smiling broadly. "I'll show you. Why don't you let me drive?"

She hesitated for only a fraction of a second before sliding over to let him in.

# 5

The restaurant was on the Santa Monica pier. It was small and cozy, the tables covered with red checked cloths and lit by candles. Theo and Toni sat by a window overlooking the bay. Nearby, they could see pelicans diving for fish, and seagulls bobbing up and down on the gentle swells. It was nearly dark now.

Dinner was over and they were lingering over coffee and brandy. There had been a tacit, if silent, agreement not to discuss anything important during the meal. Toni talked about her job and Theo mentioned some interesting assignments he'd worked on recently. Both knew there was a great deal to be said, but it would have to be done in the right way, at the right time. The time for charging headlong through defensive barriers was over. Both were nervous about this meeting, more nervous than they'd been the first night they met. This was their second chance with each other, and each understood that after this, there would be no more chances.

"This place is marvelous. How did you find it?" Toni asked, taking another sip of after-dinner coffee.

"Since I live out of hotel rooms wherever I go, I tend to

64

eat in a lot of restaurants. I can tell you the best and worst places in most of the major cities of the world."

"I've lived in L.A. for years, but somehow I never got around to coming to the pier. It's nice."

"Actually, it's not a terrific place after dark. There are a lot of winos and a truly mind-boggling assortment of weirdos. But the food's great, and if you come early enough, there's a terrific view."

Smiling wryly, Toni responded, "You're always the harsh realist, aren't you?"

"Photographers are realists by nature. After all, the camera doesn't lie," he bantered, smiling back at her.

Seeing that flash of devastating grin that softened his features and made him look boyishly charming made Toni's heart melt as it had done on that dark Chelsea street a month earlier. It's only infatuation, she reminded herself forcefully, trying to regain control of her battered emotions. But infatuation, she had to admit, was a potent force.

"Reality doesn't have to be grim. It can be beautiful," she insisted.

"I think we've had this argument before," Theo said pointedly.

Embarrassed at being reminded of London, Toni tried to change the subject rather obviously. "So, are you working on an assignment right now?"

"Yeah, I'm doing a series on Vietnamese refugees who've settled in Orange County. It's for the *Saturday Evening Post.*"

"That sounds interesting."

"It's pretty quiet, anyway. After a month in Northern Ireland, I decided I wanted to go somewhere where people aren't throwing bombs and shooting each other."

"Will you be here long?" Toni finally asked, reluctant to show too avid an interest in his schedule, but too curious to resist.

"What you're getting at is, am I going to be taking off in the morning," Theo interpreted frankly.

"Well, you have been known to disappear as inexplicably as the proverbial rabbit in a magician's hat," Toni responded just as frankly.

Theo laughed deeply. "Touché." Then, "I'll be here for at least a month, maybe much longer. I'm thinking about setting up a temporary base in L.A. It's convenient for getting back and forth to El Salvador. *Time* magazine has asked me to cover the war down there. But it's a fitful situation. They go for weeks at a time with relative peace, then fighting breaks out and you have to get there fast to cover it."

"I see," Toni said thoughtfully, digesting the interesting information that Theo might be around for quite awhile. She wasn't entirely sure how she felt about that.

Watching her carefully, Theo continued slowly, "And I have to admit there are other considerations for staying around here."

Toni wasn't coy enough to ask exactly what he meant. She *knew*. She and Theo were beyond coy pretense now.

"Don't you get tired of covering wars?" she asked curiously.

"It isn't exactly fun, I'll admit. But it seems to be what I do best." Then he asked, "How about you? Do you like your job?"

"Most of the time, I love it. I didn't actually start out to be a television reporter. When I left my husband, I wasn't sure what I wanted to do. I only knew that I needed to have my own accomplishments. I couldn't live vicariously through someone else's success anymore. An old friend from college, Carol Bellini, offered me a job at the television station where she had been working. She was very honest about it. The station manager wanted me because I had a name and some minor notoriety as the wife of a celebrity. I'd appeared on a lot of television talk shows and in magazine layouts with Robert."

Toni smiled and continued, "But Carol thought I could amount to a pretty decent reporter. I've worked hard to prove she was right. Now, I can't imagine doing anything else. But it can be infuriating sometimes. Even in this day and age, it's hard for a woman reporter to be taken seriously, to be allowed to cover the hard-news stories; at least on the local level. And there's the problem of age. You get over the hill fast."

Theo looked surprised. "You could almost pass for a teenager. How on earth can you talk about being over the hill?"

Toni laughed drily. "I'll be twenty-nine soon. And in this business, that's *old*. Most of the women reporters at the station are younger than I am. Unfortunately, the career of a television newswoman has little to do with intellect, knowledge of current events or field experience in journalism. What's crucial is a youthful and attractive appearance. Obviously, that's a quality that slips away the longer a woman stays in the business. If you're ambitious enough to want to become an anchorwoman, as I do, you can forget about it after forty."

"But look at Charles Kuralt and Walter Cronkite," Theo interrupted.

"They're *men*. It's okay for men to have wrinkles. I guess it's considered cuddly or reassuring somehow. But women have to be young and pretty; at least on the local level. On the national level, it's much better. There, they care about what you can do much more than how you look."

"I assume you're interested in making it to a network, then?"

"Of course. I want to go as far as I can. And I certainly don't want to be a has-been at forty."

Theo looked at Toni, her face glowing in the soft

candlelight. "It's impossible to think of you as old. There's something intrinsically youthful and endearing about you. Even your eyes are quick and bright and curious."

Toni grew embarrassed under his compliments. She responded, "I suspect you're the sort of man who doesn't think a woman should be ambitious."

"No. I think women who have stimulating careers are much more interesting than women who are interested only in themselves. But from what I've seen, it's hard for a woman to have a career and a happy personal life."

For a moment, Toni wasn't sure if that was a pointed reference to her marriage.

Suddenly realizing what he'd said, Theo hurried to explain. "I'm sorry. I wasn't referring to your marriage. I forgot about that."

"It's okay. The truth is, I found it impossible to have a career and a marriage, but I don't think the divorce was really a result of my ambition. I think women *can* have it all, but the men in their lives have to be willing to give more than they're used to giving. They have to share in the responsibilities around the house, especially with children."

"Do you want kids?" Theo asked unexpectedly.

Taken aback, Toni answered hesitantly, "Well . . . yes, very much."

Then, determined to put Theo on the defensive, she asked, "How about you? Do you want children?"

Theo smiled. "You like turning the tables on me, don't you?"

"All's fair in love and war," Toni answered quickly. Then, realizing what she'd said, she was embarrassed. Recovering her poise, she finished, "And we've already established that you know a great deal about both."

To her relief, Theo looked a bit embarrassed this time. His psychological armor was thick, and his confidence bordered on arrogance. But he was human enough to be slightly unsettled when a woman whose opinion he valued told him, in a roundabout way, that she thought he was a terrific lover.

"I'd like to have kids," he finally answered. "My brothers have half a dozen between them. I've always gotten along well with my nieces and nephews. Better than with my brothers, in fact. The kids think what I do is exciting. My brothers think it's crazy."

Toni smiled in understanding. "I've seen that problem a lot with my friends, especially women who've chosen a career over having kids. But I never had it myself. My grandmother, who raised me, was a journalist herself, and always encouraged me to enter that field. She's a Calvinist basically. She thinks all experience is the route to self-improvement. She taught me to take every lesson that could be taken, to learn everything that could be learned. When I told her I was marrying Robert and not pursuing a career, she was actually disappointed."

"She must be an unusual person."

"Oh, she *is,*" Toni responded enthusiastically. "I've never met anyone else like her. If I accomplish half as much in my life as she's done, I'll be satisfied. Perhaps you've heard of her—her name's Leonie Vallis."

"Of course. Leonie Vallis is a legend in the news business. She's been around for ages, hasn't she?"

"She started with the Lindbergh kidnapping case and really made a name for herself with the abdication of King Edward VIII of England. She's nearly eighty now, but she's got more energy than I do. She smokes awful Portuguese cigarettes and drinks exotic teas. She's met just about every famous person in the last fifty years. Until about ten years ago when she developed a heart problem, she was still actively working. Now she's retired and living in a beautiful old Spanish estate in Santa Barbara."

"I'd love to meet her."

Toni hesitated. Meeting one's family usually had serious overtones. And her current relationship with Theo wasn't headed in that direction. On the other hand, she knew that he and Leonie would enjoy each other enormously. Don't be so skittish, she told herself finally. We're talking about an innocent get-together, no strings attached.

"Okay," she said finally. "Maybe someday we can go up there. It's a lovely drive along the coast."

"When?" Theo pressed.

"Well . . ." Toni thought hurriedly. "How about three weeks from now? On Saturday. We could go up in the morning, spend the afternoon and leave after dinner."

"Sounds great. I'll call you the day before to set up an exact time."

Toni glanced up sharply.

Theo caught her look. He finished, grinning wryly, "I *promise* I'll call."

"Okay." Then, trying hard to fill the sudden silence, Toni said, "So, tell me about this assignment. Have you met many of the refugees yet?"

Putting down his brandy, Theo responded seriously, "I think it's time we got past the small talk. Not that it hasn't been enjoyable. I *like* talking to you. But there are some more things that need to be said."

"I see." Toni looked down, her hands nervously tracing invisible patterns on the tablecloth. "Let's go outside, shall we? I've always hated having serious discussions in restaurants. They're just not private enough, somehow."

"Okay."

Theo called the waiter over and quickly paid the bill.

Outside, the pier was nearly empty. They walked silently down the length of it until they got to the end. Toni leaned over the worn wood railing, looking out to sea. The mild breeze tossed her hair and she reached up to push back an errant curl that was brushing her cheek softly.

Earlier, she'd bitterly accused Theo of running away, of being dishonest. Now she found herself sorely tempted to bolt like a frightened filly. It gave her a glimmer of understanding of how Theo must have felt in London, confronted with something he didn't expect and wasn't prepared to deal with.

I'm *afraid,* she thought, admitting it to herself for the first time. It amazed and troubled her.

During her entire marriage to Robert, she'd never felt so afraid. The relationship had never touched her deeply enough to bring out that elemental emotion. But Theo was different. She was afraid of what he would say, and what he wouldn't. Afraid he would leave. And more afraid he would stay.

"I'm sorry I left you like that in London, as if I didn't give a damn about you," he began without hesitation.

His bluntness hurt. "We went over that. You're forgiven," Toni finally managed to say, still not looking at him. She concentrated fiercely on the horizon.

He smiled. She caught the smile out of the corner of her eye and it drew her to him. She turned to face him shyly.

"We really didn't get that settled," he insisted. "There's more to it. You were right to think what you did, because that's the way my relationships normally go. Not 'love 'em and leave 'em,' exactly. I'm not *that* crude. But definitely noninvolvement. When I first met you, I tried to tell myself that you were just another woman; exceptionally pretty, of course, with a temper that is infuriating and delightful at the same time. But still, just another woman."

He paused thoughtfully. "I guess that's been my motto—'another town, another country, another brief relationship.' I meant it when I said I never stay in one place long enough to get involved. I expected things to go the same way with you. And when they didn't, when I couldn't get you out of my mind, it shook me. I went back to Northern Ireland to finish my assignment there. And I've gotta tell you, I spent one long night in a pub drinking myself into oblivion trying to forget about you. Trying to convince myself that what happened between us meant nothing."

"You're right about what I thought," Toni responded softly. "I thought our . . . our affair meant nothing to you. And I've been trying to convince myself that it meant nothing to me, too."

"I appreciate your honesty."

"I appreciate *yours.*" Toni added, smiling broadly now, "We've gone from shouting at each other to having a mutual admiration society. It's getting downright saccharine."

"That's the first time I've seen you smile so openly. Your whole face lights up when you smile. That combination of soft sweetness and a temper that can go off like a rocket is really something."

He paused, then continued huskily, "The French have an expression for it. *Tu m'enivres.*"

"What does it mean?" she asked softly.

"You intoxicate me," he answered slowly, his eyes holding her own in a rapt gaze.

As Theo looked at Toni intently, she suddenly felt a wave of desire for him. And she knew that he felt the same thing. But this wasn't yet the time for physical intimacy. There were still important things to be said, old wounds to be tended.

"There's something else I want to say, Toni," he began, clearing his throat nervously.

She felt her body tense now. She had some idea of what was coming, and she wasn't at all sure she was ready to hear it. Their brief relationship had been a roller coaster, with terrifying lows and delirious highs. At the moment, what she wanted more than anything was to be on an even keel for a while, to take things slowly. There was much to think about already, and she didn't want to add to it.

It was time to stop probing deeply with each other, at least for a while. There was a great deal left to discover in each other, but there was also a great deal of time to do so.

"Wait. Please," she asked, laying her hand softly on his arm.

To her relief, he understood. "All right," he said finally, after a long pause. Then, putting his arm around her shoulder lightly, protectively, he led her back to the car.

They drove toward the station where Theo's rented car was parked. In the quiet of the dark car, Toni watched Theo surreptitiously out of the corner of her eye. He was concentrating on the road and unaware of her scrutiny. His strong, rugged hands gripped the wheel firmly.

Theo's hands, Toni thought wonderingly, holding the key to paradise. . . .

She mustn't let herself dwell on that, she knew, or she would be lost. She forced herself to look up at his face, in profile now as he stared ahead at the road. His profile, clean and strong, was especially appealing.

Toni had never mentally picked apart a man this way before, carefully cataloging every facet of his appearance. With Theo, however, she found herself wanting to do all sorts of things she had never done before. She felt emotions she never dreamed she possessed. The man amazed her, not so much for his intelligence or provocative sensuality, but for his mystical effect on her. He made her feel fourteen again, as if she were just discovering the magical attraction between male and female. He made her want to open herself up both emotionally and physically as she had never done with Robert. It was exhilarating and frightening, yet worrying about it was useless. For she knew that where Theo was concerned, she had no more control than a moth drawn to a flame.

Sitting in the comfortable silence that neither cared to break with unnecessary conversation, Toni longed to touch him. She wanted to trace the contours of his face, to run her fingers through his thick, wavy brown hair, to place her fingertips gently against his lips.

Instead, she held herself tightly in check.

All too soon they arrived at the parking lot. Pulling up beside his own car, he turned off the motor of Toni's. In the darkness, Toni could barely make out his expression. It was remote and unreadable. Suddenly she felt terribly nervous, and she knew perfectly well why.

What happens now? she wondered, trying to look much more composed than she felt.

She wanted to explain to Theo that he may have gotten the wrong impression of her in London. She didn't take sex lightly, had never gone to bed with a man so quickly before. And she couldn't now just hop back into bed with him, though her body ached for the sweet release that only he could give her. Everything had happened too quickly on this night. She needed time to think.

Theo seemed to be watching her, too. The moment, both agonizing and deliciously pregnant with anticipation, stretched out until Toni thought she must say something or have a nervous breakdown.

Without warning, Theo leaned over and kissed her softly on the mouth. It was the merest brushing of lips, yet it ignited her very soul. Then he whispered, "I'll be seeing you," and left.

In a matter of seconds, he had driven his car out of the

parking lot, leaving Toni sitting quietly, unable to move.

She was relieved that he hadn't pressed the matter of their sleeping together yet. It showed a sensitivity that she hadn't given him credit for possessing. Yet, part of her wished fervently that he hadn't been so damn considerate.

# 6

When Toni entered her house, the telephone was ringing insistently. Switching on a lamp, she grabbed the receiver quickly and said, "Hello," breathlessly.

"What happened?"

It was Carol, and she sounded as if she were asking Toni about a major, just-breaking news story.

"What on earth are you talking about?" Toni asked, sighing with disappointment. For no reason, she had expected it to be Theo. Pulling off her shoes, she carried the phone over to the sofa and sat down heavily. She was suddenly utterly exhausted.

"You know perfectly well what I'm talking about, Toni," Carol continued, clearly exasperated and impatient. "I *saw* you leave with that guy tonight. He's the one you met in London, isn't he?"

"Yes. How did you guess?"

Carol chuckled. "It was pretty obvious by the way you looked. Your expression was . . . well, thunderstruck. I only know one man who could possibly have that effect on you." Then, probing, "So, like a bad penny, he's shown up finally. By the way, are you alone?"

"Of course," Toni answered firmly, pulling her stockinged legs up under her comfortably. "We had dinner and I came home. *Alone.*"

"That's all?"

"Yes." Then, drily, "If you expected something more torrid, I'm sorry to disappoint you."

"Why did he show up after all this time?"

"Carol, if you weren't my closest friend, which you may not be shortly, I'd be irritated by this third degree."

"It isn't a third degree. It's merely girlish curiosity. Sounds to me as if you're a bit irritated with *him.*"

Toni couldn't help laughing. Carol was like an irresistible force when she wanted information. She always got it, one way or another. That made her a highly successful news producer, and an often exasperating friend.

"Listen," Toni explained patiently. "He happened to be in town, so he came by to see me. We had dinner. We . . . talked," she said hesitantly. Then she continued more firmly, "And we'll be going up to visit Leonie soon. That's all there is to it."

"Visiting your family, eh? That's *very* suggestive."

"Carol! He's interested in meeting Leonie because she's a fascinating person. *You* were dying to meet her when you learned I was related to her."

"I see." Carol's terse comment was full of sly innuendo.

"Listen . . ."

Before Toni could finish, Carol interrupted, "You can downplay this all you want, Toni, but you're forgetting that I knew you before you spent five years in Beverly Hills learning how to put up a façade of bored indifference. The fact is, when you first laid eyes on him tonight, you were *really* jolted."

"Carol, *enough.*"

"Okay. If you don't want to tell *me* anything, I'll tell *you* a few things."

"Such as?"

"Such as, he's *gorgeous*, and I can understand now what sent you off the beam in London."

"I appreciate your approving of my taste in men," Toni responded sarcastically.

"Actually, I never did before. Robert was an ass. But you're improving with age. And before you say something scathing about that, I want you to know that I didn't call just to tell you I think he's terrifically attractive."

"Oh?" In spite of herself, Toni was intrigued.

"When you mentioned his name before, I didn't recognize it. But when I saw him tonight, it all came back to me. I haven't actually met him but I've seen him a couple of times."

"Where?"

"Oh, just around."

For the first time, Carol sounded evasive. Immediately, Toni sensed that there was something Carol didn't want to say.

"All I'm getting at is that I've heard the guy really plays the field." There was an awkward silence before Carol finished hesitantly, "I just wanted you to know."

"You're not telling me anything I don't already know," Toni finally managed to say. She was no longer angry at Carol. Carol was her oldest friend, and they had long ago reached the point of being completely honest with each other. What bothered Toni now was the feeling that there was more that Carol might tell her, but was somehow reluctant to do so.

She decided to come right out with her suspicions. Carol was a rotten liar, especially with Toni. "So, what is it you don't want to tell me?"

"What?"

"Don't be coy. It isn't your style. There's something on your mind. Now, what is it?"

"I just wanted to let you know the guy's quite a Casanova," Carol protested unconvincingly.

"Sure. And pigs fly."

"Toni . . ."

"*What* is it, Carol?" Toni was growing angry again. She'd had about enough of the entire conversation.

"All right. It isn't any big thing. You asked where I saw him before. Well, I saw him with Gayle Gerard several times, here and in New York. As I understand it, they've had a thing going for quite awhile. Very casual, no strings attached, you do your thing and I'll do mine."

"And Gayle is in L.A.," Toni added soberly.

"Well . . . yeah," Carol finished, clearly uncomfortable. She continued anxiously, "Listen, Toni, it doesn't *mean* anything, and that's why I didn't want to tell you. God knows, they're not engaged or anything. And he's not the only guy Gayle's been seeing."

"I understand what you're trying to say," Toni responded softly. "But, Carol, I'm awfully tired, so I'll see you tomorrow, okay?"

"Sure. Are you all right?"

"Terrific." Her tone was flat.

"Theo Chakiris *is* gorgeous," Carol repeated enthusiastically. "Enjoy it, *whatever* he offers, for as long as it lasts."

"Carol, I don't want to be rude, but I'm not in the mood for advice right now."

"Sorry. I won't say another word. Well, maybe one more word—good night."

"Good night."

After hanging up the phone, Toni continued sitting on the sofa for a long time. The house was in shadows because she hadn't bothered to turn on more than one dim lamp. The cautious optimism she'd felt as she hurried into the house earlier was gone now. Why did it have to be Gayle? she wondered bitterly. Toni had met her only once, briefly, and Gayle had treated her with disdain. Toni was, after all, only a local reporter.

Though she tried not to, Toni couldn't help envisioning

Theo with Gayle. What a stunning pair they would make, both tall and attractive, with that same sardonic gleam in their eyes. Toni couldn't avoid assuming the obvious—that Theo was in L.A. not to see her but to be with Gayle.

I was probably merely an afterthought, Toni thought unhappily.

Pulling her knees up, she rested her chin on them, and wrapped her arms around her legs. She stared, unseeing, into the empty fireplace, her mind a confusion of jumbled thoughts.

It was hardly a coincidence that Gayle was in L.A. at the same time as Theo. Yet on the other hand, he hadn't pressed the issue of sex.

Surely, she thought, if that was all he was interested in, he would have been more persistent. After all, he must be aware of the effect he had on her.

Shaking her head irritably, Toni said to herself, I'm just not going to worry about it. I have better things to do with my time, she insisted silently, than worry about Theo Chakiris' motives.

She went to bed then, determined not to think any more about Theo or Gayle. But her sleep, when it finally came, was filled with erotic dreams about a dark-eyed man.

# 7

Theo called two days later. Toni was in the newsroom, concentrating on writing a story that Carol insisted she needed in a hurry. When the phone rang, Toni answered it mechanically, her attention still on the half-empty sheet in the typewriter.

"Toni, it's Theo."

His voice had the immediate effect of jolting her out of her concentration. As she answered, "Yes," hesitantly, she wished she had been more prepared for this.

"Are you busy?" he asked, detecting the restraint in her voice.

"Well, yes, as a matter of fact, I'm in the middle of a rush story. But I can spare a minute."

"I won't keep you then. How about dinner tomorrow night?"

"Oh," Toni said stupidly, hating herself for not being able to come up with a quick, firm answer. "All right," she finally agreed. It had only taken an instant to realize that she wanted to see him again very much.

"Is anything wrong?" he asked slowly.

"No, I'm just preoccupied with this story," Toni lied.

"Okay. I'll let you go then. Can I pick you up at seven?"

"Could you make it eight? I don't get home until about seven."

"Sure. What's your address?"

When she told him, he said, "Ah, you live at the beach. Must be nice."

"It is."

"Well, I won't keep you. See you tomorrow."

When he'd hung up, Toni sat there for a long moment, thinking hard. She simply couldn't go on feeling so awkward with him. At that moment she made a decision to forget about Gayle. She wouldn't let Carol's gossip spoil her time with Theo. Whatever would happen, would happen. *Que sera, sera,* she told herself drily. Then she once more began typing the story.

Theo stepped into Toni's house precisely at eight o'clock and was immediately impressed with the atmosphere. It was cheerfully unpretentious, like Toni herself. Though everything was in harmony, it wasn't the rigid orchestration of a professional interior decorator, but the natural harmony of a creative personality.

Then he turned to look at Toni herself. She was wearing a cream-colored silk blouse flecked with violet, with a violet yoke and piped with silvery metal and ribbons. The willowy silk skirt was violet foulard deeply banded with more violet. Her hair was pulled up severely in back with a tortoise-shell comb, but in front a froth of curls cascaded over her forehead.

Toni turned after closing the door behind him, and said merrily, "Good evening, Mr. Chakiris."

"Good evening, Ms. Lawrence."

He smiled, then appraised her appreciatively for a

moment longer. Finally he handed her the bouquet of flowers he'd been holding.

"I love lilacs," Toni said, sniffing them happily. She disappeared into the kitchen for a moment, then returned with the flowers in a tall, clear vase. After putting them on the coffee table in front of the fireplace, she turned to face Theo.

"Would you like a drink before we leave?"

If he was surprised that she wasn't hurrying him out of there, he didn't show it.

"Yes, thanks. Scotch, if you have it."

"Oh, I have just about everything. The first time Leonie came to visit me here she was disappointed to discover that I had no liquor in the house. So she immediately went out and bought enough to keep your average alcoholic happy for a year. She said she wanted to be able to come here without feeling she was back in the days of prohibition."

Toni opened the liquor cabinet and poured his drink. When she handed it to him, their hands brushed for the briefest second. Theo was startled by the jolt of electricity that seemed to race through his body. Trying hard to conceal the fact that his every nerve had come alive, he said, "It's perfect."

He was grateful for the calming effect of the stiff drink.

Picking up a glass of wine sitting on a nearby table, Toni said easily, "Let's sit down, shall we?"

He followed her to the sofa and was amused to see her choose an armchair. So, she was a bit nervous, despite her air of relaxed friendliness. It touched him somehow to think she was reluctant to sit close to him.

"Where are we going tonight?" Toni asked, sipping the wine slowly.

"A Japanese restaurant high up in the Hollywood Hills. It's called Yamashiro's. Have you heard of it?"

"Yes. It has a marvelous view, doesn't it?"

"Right. And the food's almost as good as the view. Have you been there?"

"No." Then, wryly, "You seem to have a knack for introducing me to new things."

Suddenly realizing the full import of her innocent observation, she blushed furiously.

Theo responded with a quiet half-smile. Looking around the room, and comparing it to the vivid young woman sitting opposite him, he decided they were in perfect harmony. "You have a terrific home."

"Thanks. Leonie helped me furnish it with some of her cast-off antiques. Even her castoffs are beautiful, though. In all of her travels throughout the world, she made a point of buying antiques. It got to the point where they were stacked up in her garage in Santa Barbara. So when I moved in here, she simply showed up one day with a moving van full of furniture." She laughed. "I didn't have nearly enough room for it all."

Theo was aware that Toni was trying to keep the small talk going for as long as possible. The atmosphere between them was electric with anticipation. But they had made love the first time without really knowing each other. And he sensed that Toni wanted to get to know him now, and for him to know her, before they explored each other's bodies again.

When he finished his drink, he set the glass on the table. "We'd better be going," he said, glancing at his watch. "Our reservation's for nine, and we've just barely got enough time to make it."

A look of relief crossed Toni's face before she smiled and said, "I'm ready. Let's go."

The drive up Pacific Coast Highway was quiet. In the dimness of the late summer evening, the ocean was a vague mass of black, edged with silver-tipped waves lapping at the shore. Though neither said very much, each was intensely aware of the other's presence.

At the restaurant, they ate on a broad patio that afforded a stunning view of the Los Angeles basin. Below them, L.A. was a vast carpet of lights spreading into infinity. The food was large, succulent shrimp and fresh vegetables prepared *tempura* style, fried in a light, crisp batter. It was delicious.

Theo and Toni talked about a variety of subjects, discovering surprisingly similar views on everything from religion to politics. They were silent when they felt like it, and it was a comfortable silence. They were getting to know each other, not as lovers this time, but as friends; exploring each other's minds and hearts before once more exploring each other's bodies. Their courting was slow, cautious, yet tinged with a delicious anticipation of where it might all ultimately lead. Behind their mutual revelations about likes and dislikes lay the mystery and sexual magnetism that had driven them into each other's arms in London. It was even more powerful now, this force that neither could yet admit might be love.

"What was it like growing up in San Francisco?" Toni asked, setting down her teacup and smiling up at Theo.

"Don't laugh, but what I remember most is the smell of fish. We lived close to the docks and the smell was everywhere. Especially when my father came home at night. He always smelled of fish. My mother used to make him take a bath before eating dinner. She said she didn't want her roast lamb smelling like tuna.

At that moment, Theo felt less guarded than he had felt in a long while.

"You loved your mother very much, didn't you?" Toni said quietly.

Theo withdrew from this delicate subject, his open look replaced by the usual, hardened one.

"She died when I was eight. Most of my memories of her are pretty vague. I remember the thing about the fish because it happened every night."

"I'm *so* sorry," Toni said.

Theo knew her sympathy was deeply felt, since she had borne the same loss herself. But he brushed away her sympathy gruffly. "It was a long time ago." Determined to change the subject, he continued, "What was it like for you growing up in Santa Barbara?"

Toni answered, smiling gently, "I suppose it was unusual compared to the lives most people lead. Leonie was not your average grandmother, baking cookies and reading fairy tales. For one thing, she *hated* to cook. She felt it was a waste of her time, so she left it up to a succession of cooks of widely different backgrounds. By the time I was ten, I had learned how to ask for waffles for breakfast in five languages."

Theo smiled. He was aware that she was purposefully trying to lighten the mood that had turned too serious, and he was grateful.

Toni continued, "Until I was about sixteen, Leonie was still working and traveled a lot. She took me with her when she could, but during school I had to stay home. She was quite stubborn about my not missing school. From the very beginning, she was determined that I was going to get the education that she herself had missed. She came of age at a time when girls were supposed to think about getting married and not about having careers. So she was basically self-taught."

"Who looked after you while she was gone?"

"Oh, friends, mainly. Leonie has more friends than anyone in the entire world. She always saw to it that I was well taken care of." Toni rested her arms on the table and continued nostalgically, cupping her chin in her hands, "You know, when I was very young, I thought she was more like a fairy godmother than a grandmother. She gave me the most marvelous presents and did the most incredible things. Life with her was always interesting. And there was so much *love*. She told me once about a saying the French have, that is basically, 'spend all your kisses.' She said that it means you should give all the love you have and not keep any hidden away inside; because love, unlike money, is wasted if it's not shared."

Feeling suddenly sly, Theo said slowly, "I don't want to be wasteful. Let's spend a kiss now before we're accused of hoarding."

The table was small. He had only to lean over to kiss Toni gently, lingeringly. Only their lips met; their hands remained on the table, and their bodies were separated by it. Yet it was an incredibly sensuous experience that left both breathless and dazed.

A Japanese waiter passing their table smiled, then moved on.

As they finished their strong, hot tea, Toni looked pensively at the tiny leaves at the bottom of the white porcelain cup. She said idly, "I wonder how one reads tea leaves?"

"Are you curious about your future?" Theo asked, smiling.

"Perhaps it's better to be taken by surprise," Toni replied, meeting his level gaze.

Suddenly, as they looked deep into each other's eyes, brown eyes meeting violet ones in perfect understanding, they knew that the time for waiting had passed.

"Let's go," Theo said softly, his voice almost a whisper.

Toni said nothing while Theo paid the bill and led her out to the car.

They drove for several minutes before Theo turned the car into the underground garage of his hotel.

"This is the L'Hermitage Hotel, isn't it?" Toni asked, surprised.

"Yeah."

"I didn't realize freelance photographers made enough to afford the most exclusive hotel in Beverly Hills," she said teasingly.

"War is profitable," Theo responded simply. "Maybe that's why the world can't seem to get rid of it."

Inside, they took an elevator to the fourth floor. They walked a short way down a plushly carpeted hallway before stopping at a door. Theo didn't use a key, but merely punched some buttons near the door handle. Like magic, the door unlocked. Seeing Toni's curious look, he explained, "You're given a secret combination when you check in here. It's less trouble than bothering with a key."

The room was a two-story townhouse suite, with a living room and kitchen on the first floor and a bedroom on the second. It was lavishly furnished and as big as many luxury apartments.

Raising one eyebrow quizzically, Toni commented, "Somehow, I imagined you would lean more toward inexpensive motels."

Smiling, Theo answered, "I like to be comfortable when I can be. It makes up for too many nights spent on the cold, hard ground during assignments." Then, walking up to a bar, he asked over his shoulder, "Want a drink?"

"Yes," Toni said quickly.

He poured each of them a small brandy in exquisite, cut-glass crystal brandy snifters. Handing one to Toni, he took her arm lightly and led her toward the sofa.

They sat in silence, each sipping the brandy slowly.

"I . . ." Toni started to say something, then stopped.

Theo could see that she was all nerves. Suddenly he was overwhelmed with tenderness for her, at the same time that he felt his body stir with budding excitement.

"Here," he said, taking her glass and setting it down on the table, along with his own. "You don't need that."

Rising, he pulled her up to him, then picked her up as easily as if she weighed no more than a feather. Slowly, he carried her up the stairs to the dim bedroom, lit only by the light of the moon shining through an open window. Laying her down on the bed, he whispered gently, "Don't worry, love, it will be all right."

Toni smiled in understanding.

He went slowly with her. He knew women well, and he wanted to bring to bear every ounce of that knowledge, that expertise, with this woman. He had been surprised earlier at his feelings of tenderness toward her. He didn't often feel that way toward women. Now, he was surprised that he was concerned more with her pleasure than his own. Though he always made a point of leaving women fulfilled, he did so in a detached sort of way, more for his ego's sake, than theirs. But with Toni, it was deeply important to him that she not be frightened or hurried. He wanted her to savor the pleasures of their lovemaking as profoundly as he did.

In London, her obvious innocence had made him take care with her. Now, his realization that he had the power to hurt her deeply because she cared so much for him moved him in the same way.

He undressed her slowly, gently kissing each new area of exposed skin. When she was naked, he let his gaze wander over her tiny, exquisite body, taking in the soft curves, the fullness of her small, perfect breasts, the hollow at the base of her long, slender throat.

Her body was a feast for his eyes, and he knew he could look at it forever without growing bored.

As he started to unbutton his shirt, Toni reached up and stayed his hand. "No. Let me do it." Smiling a slow, provocative grin, she finished, "I'm not quite so inexperienced now, you see."

Her fingers were awkward at first, but he didn't mind. He found it endearing. She learned quickly, though, how to deal with his garments, and soon he, too, was naked. He found her eagerness highly stimulating, and it grew more and more difficult to restrain himself. At that moment there was nothing in the world that he wanted more than Antonia Lawrence. He wanted to meld her body to his, to make her part of him.

When her full lower lip trembled slightly as he moved over her, he whispered hoarsely, "Don't be afraid."

"I'm not afraid," she responded breathlessly.

He knew then how much she wanted him, and he waited no longer to possess her.

# 8

〜〜〜〜〜〜〜

The following weeks were warm and sunny. Theo and Toni spent more and more time together, getting to know each other. Their separate lives continued as before. Both were dedicated to their work. There were days when they were so busy that they didn't see each other but only talked on the telephone. But their lives began to merge more and more as time passed, until finally Theo was spending almost no time at his hotel.

They shared quiet dinners at Toni's house, followed by long walks down the beach. Occasionally, they spent the night at Theo's hotel, merely to keep up the pretense that they weren't really living together.

Waking up in the morning with Toni was a complete delight for Theo. She brought him croissants and coffee in bed, then teased him playfully in the shower until he took her beneath the warm spray of water.

For Toni, sleeping with Theo was a profoundly secure feeling. He held her in his arms all night. And though she gloried in his lovemaking, the times she loved best were when he caressed her tenderly without demanding anything further.

One evening Toni walked into her house just as the telephone rang. Putting down the bags of groceries she was carrying, she hurriedly picked up the receiver.

"Hello," she said eagerly. Theo was away for the night on an extended photo session, and she was hoping the caller was he.

"You sound like you're expecting to hear from someone," the caller said drily.

"Oh, Leonie," Toni said, genuinely glad to hear from her grandmother, but disappointed that it wasn't Theo.

"I just wanted to make sure you didn't fall off the face of the earth. I haven't heard from you in ages, Toni."

"I know and I'm sorry. I've been . . . well, busy." Then, before Leonie could ask the probing, perceptive questions that she was so adept at, Toni explained in a rush, "I'm going to come up this weekend, though. And I'll be bringing someone with me. Someone I especially want you to meet."

"Somehow, that doesn't come as a complete surprise, young lady," Leonie responded brusquely. "I didn't think you'd been spending all your time working. So who is this person?"

"His name is Theodopolus Chakiris . . ."

"Ah, a young man."

"*Leonie,* don't jump to conclusions," Toni said firmly.

"The last time you brought a man to meet me, you married him. Unfortunately," Leonie commented tersely.

"That was seven years ago."

"I'm perfectly aware of how long it's been. I'm not senile, you know."

Toni laughed. "You're the last person I would accuse of senility." Then, trying to make her words sound casual, but unable to keep a nervous note out of her voice, she continued, "He's just a very good friend. I . . . I hope you like him."

"I'm sure I shall. After Robert, anyone is bound to be an improvement."

"Leonie!"

"Is he attractive?" Leonie asked frankly.

"Terribly."

"Good. He'll do more for my blood pressure, then, than all the pills my damn doctor keeps shoving at me."

Toni laughed happily. "We'll see you Saturday," she finished. "And try not to be an old dragon."

"Who, me?" Leonie asked with mock sweetness, before saying good-bye.

Toni felt exhilarated by the call. She was sure that Leonie would like Theo as much as she did.

Just minutes later, when Theo called, Toni was still feeling euphoric. "I talked with Leonie tonight," she announced as soon as Theo said hello. "I told her I'm bringing a very attractive man to meet her."

There was a brief silence which surprised Toni. One of the nicest things about Theo was the way she could laugh with him. But this time he wasn't responding to her teasing.

"Uh, Toni, about Saturday . . ." he began hesitantly.

It wasn't like Theo to sound embarrassed, and Toni immediately suspected that something was wrong.

"What about it?" she asked, her tone wary now.

"Something has come up here and I'm not going to get back to town by Saturday. Could we possibly go up to see your grandmother next weekend?"

When Toni said nothing, Theo continued, "You know I wouldn't cancel it if I could avoid it. I was looking forward to Saturday. And I hope it won't be a problem for her to put things off."

"Don't worry about it, Theo," Toni said flatly. "Listen, I have to go now. There's someone at the door," she lied.

"Toni . . ." Theo began, then stopped helplessly. "Okay, I'll call you Sunday."

"I may be gone," Toni answered. It was a lie, but as soon as she said it, she decided to make it the truth. She would go somewhere, *anywhere*, rather than wait for his call. She knew perfectly well why he was canceling their date Saturday. Just that morning she had heard that Gayle Gerard was coming back to town that weekend. Theo was probably going to be with Gayle.

"I'll call you anyway," Theo insisted.

"Whatever you like. I really have to go."

The conversation had totally disintegrated. A few minutes earlier she had been happy to hear from him. Now, she couldn't wait to hang up the telephone.

"Good-bye," she said curtly.

For a long time she simply sat by the phone, staring at it as if it were a malignant force. Then she rose and went into the kitchen. Methodically, she began putting away the groceries she had just carried in. Tears misted her lovely violet eyes, but she fought them back. She wasn't going to give in to self-pity. She wouldn't let any man, even one with the most beautiful brown eyes she'd ever seen, make her cry again. She'd had five years of that with Robert, and five years was more than enough.

By the time the groceries were put away, her eyes were dry and her attitude was firmly set. Theo Chakiris could go happily to hell, with her blessings. She didn't intend to see him again.

On Sunday morning, Toni woke up to the insistent ringing of the telephone. Her hand reached out to grab the receiver before she realized who was probably calling her so early. Letting the phone ring, she counted nine rings before it finally stopped. Then she relaxed back against the pillow. And contrary to her firm resolve, she cried her heart out.

Finally, she rose and unplugged the phone while she quickly showered and dressed. She couldn't bear to listen to it ring again.

Outside, she put down the top of her convertible, then drove south along the coast highway. She had no particular destination in mind. But she didn't go north because she knew she couldn't face her grandmother. Leonie had asked persistent questions when Toni called to cancel their get-together. It was all Toni could do to get off the phone without breaking down and telling her the unhappy story behind the cancellation.

The highway was nearly deserted this early on a Sunday morning. Toni felt the cool ocean breeze whip her loose curls against her cheeks and forehead. Late in the morning she stopped for lunch at a seaside restaurant. Though the chowder was thick with succulent morsels of clams and the French bread that accompanied it was crisp and tasty, she barely touched it. She had little appetite.

Realizing that she was going to end up in Mexico shortly, she turned the car back toward L.A.

During the drive back to the city, she thought about Theo objectively. From the beginning, he had been completely honest with her, making no promises, asking her for nothing more than he himself was willing to give.

You knew what to expect, she told herself firmly. There's no reason to be surprised when he acts in character.

She realized it was stupid of her to have assumed he might have changed, simply because they got along so well together. Obviously, their relationship meant something quite different to her than it meant to him.

When she reached the city late in the afternoon, she went to a movie that barely captured her attention. Then she forced herself to eat a dinner that she didn't enjoy. Finally, she returned home, feeling utterly forlorn.

She parked her car in the garage, which was level with the highway. As she started down the steep brick steps that led to her front door on the beach level, she realized that someone was sitting on her front doorstep. It took only a moment to recognize the familiar outlines of Theo's body.

At her approach, he rose, dusting off the seat of his trousers. "Hello," he said naturally, as if their last conversation hadn't ended on an ice-cold note.

Toni asked bluntly, "What do you want?" as she took out her house key.

"Obviously, I want to talk to you," Theo responded.

"Well, it's late and I'm awfully tired, so if you don't mind . . ." Toni began.

She was cut off by Theo's firm, "Yes, I *do* mind." As she opened the door, he finished, "So, if it's all right with you, I'll just come inside where we can at least talk to each other in the light. I can hardly see your face."

Toni was glad for the moonless night. She didn't want Theo to see the effect his presence had on her. But it was clear he didn't intend to leave without talking to her. And she decided that might be best, after all, however painful it would be. At least then, things would be definitely over, with no lingering questions.

"All right. But this will have to be quick."

Inside, Toni dropped her key back into her purse and set it down on a table. Then, without asking Theo if he would like a drink, without even inviting him to sit down, she said, "What is it that's so important it can't wait?"

She was unbearably tired and it was an effort to maintain an aura of calm disinterest.

Outside, the surf was pounding heavily against the shore. A Santa Ana wind had come up with the setting of the sun, and the wind was whipping the dark waves into a frenzy. The high, keening wind and the furious surf seemed to Toni to reflect the atmosphere inside the house.

Theo shifted nervously on his feet, thrusting his hands in the pockets of his denim jacket. Then, forcing a smile, he began, "I just wanted to apologize."

"For what?" Toni asked curtly.

"For canceling our date yesterday. Apparently it meant a great deal to you, this thing about meeting your grandmother."

Toni's eyebrows arched as she asked, "And what makes you think it meant so much to me?"

This was too much for Theo. He exploded, "Damn it, Toni, you're obviously mad as hell at me! And you've been that way since we talked the other night!" Then, calming down, he finished, "I didn't want to cancel our date, you know. Believe it or not, I was looking forward to meeting your grandmother."

Toni's rigid control of her temper snapped. Her eyes blazed a deep gentian violet as she responded with all the pent up hurt and anger that she had been keeping inside for several days. "I don't give a damn what your feelings are about Leonie," she exploded.

Theo was clearly taken aback at her outburst. "Wait a minute. Something else is wrong here, isn't it?" He tried to reach out to Toni, to take her hand, but she pulled away. Crossing the room, she stood in front of the windows, looking out at the black, storm-tossed waves.

She held her small shoulders rigid, her whole manner reflecting her stubborn pride.

"Just go away," she said more quietly now.

She hadn't bothered to turn on more than one lamp. In the darkness, the furniture was only shadows. The entire mood was somber and depressing.

"No, I won't go away. *Ever*," Theo said with emphasis, surprising Toni with the heartfelt emotion in his voice.

She stiffened, and for a moment it seemed that she was going to turn and face him. But she remained looking out at the ocean. "I don't want you here, Theo," she said dully.

"All right, if you really want me to go, I will," he said. Then, he added sternly, "But there's something I want to know first. Tell me what I've done to break us apart so suddenly."

Toni's arms were crossed in front of her, holding herself rigidly, to keep from breaking down completely in front of him. It was hurting even more than she had expected it to. It was so hard, standing near him, wanting more than anything to feel his arms around her. Until the moment when she saw him sitting on her doorstep she hadn't fully realized what it would mean to cut him out of her life, after making him the center of it.

Now, she knew. It meant never hearing that deep, wryly mocking, yet at times curiously gentle voice. It meant never looking into those deep brown eyes that held so many secrets, so much deep feeling that he tried hard not to reveal. It meant never feeling his hands caress her body in all the intimate places he'd come to know so well.

The pain was suddenly too much to bear and she knew she was going to say things she would regret. She had hoped he would let it end without a scene, without bringing her to this point where she was driven to tell him the truth.

Oh, God, I don't want him to know how hurt I am because then he'll know how much I love him, she told herself desperately.

All she had left now was her pride and that was dangerously close to being lost. She had sworn to herself that she would play the game his way, not talking of love or commitment. Don't let me make a fool of myself in front of him, she prayed fervently, shutting her eyes tightly.

"I have the right to know why you're shutting me out of your life so abruptly," Theo went on fiercely, his own temper close to breaking now.

And then she said the words that immediately made her despise herself. "You were with Gayle yesterday." Oh, God, let me die right now, she thought hopelessly, because I've let him see that I'm jealous. That I care too much to share him with another woman. That I love him.

In a second, Theo was across the room, pulling Toni roughly to face him. To her amazement, he was smiling. It wasn't his usual sardonic grin, but a warm, relieved, happy smile. She couldn't bear it. As he pulled her to him, she buried her face in his chest, feeling the rough material of the denim jacket scrape her cheek. She thought she would never be able to look into his eyes again. Her pride was utterly devastated.

Theo's hand caressed her hair as gently as if he were petting a kitten. "Toni, honey . . ." His words were soothing. Somehow, they made her feel that all wasn't lost. But despite the reassurance of his tone, she couldn't see how things could possibly go on after this.

"I adore you," he said tenderly.

Toni was so startled, she thought at first she must have heard him wrong. Through the tears that blurred her eyes and glistened on her cheeks, she asked tentatively, "What?"

Theo entwined his fingers in her hair, then gently pulled her head back so that she looked up at him. "I adore you," he repeated clearly. Then he bent down and kissed her deeply, with a passion that was only barely under control.

Though her mind was reeling and confused, her body responded to his hungry lips and urgent hands. When he finally let her go, she breathed deeply, then began awkwardly, "But . . ."

"I know. But what about Gayle," he said quickly. His hands were roaming her body now, lightly moving up and down her back and tracing the outline of her breasts and hips. "This explanation will be brief because I don't think I can keep myself from undressing you and taking you into the bedroom much longer." He leaned down to kiss the side of her throat. Involuntarily, she arched her neck toward him.

"I did see Gayle yesterday," he whispered as his lips brushed her throat.

The moment she heard the words, Toni felt her body go limp and her heart sink. The hope that had sprung up so suddenly, just as suddenly died. So it *was* true. Before she could say a word, Theo continued evenly, "She got into town yesterday and I saw her immediately. I wanted to tell her that I wouldn't be seeing her again. I felt it was important to end the relationship right away. It could be awkward if she called my hotel room while we were together, or if we ran into her somewhere. I didn't want her to intrude on our relationship in any way."

He ran one finger lightly down her back. She felt it through the thin material of her blouse and she shivered in response.

"You mean . . ." she began.

"I mean, my relationship with Gayle is *over*. It was only a casual affair to begin with, but I didn't want it to affect what we have. Which is definitely *not* casual."

Relief mingled with intense embarrassment inside Toni's mind. She felt as if a giant weight had been lifted from her shoulders. Yet at the same time, she knew she had badly misjudged Theo and she felt horribly ashamed. No apology, she felt, could ever make up for her unkind treatment of him. But somehow, she knew, she would have to try to apologize.

"Oh, Theo, I feel like such a damn fool! I'm so sorry. I can imagine what you must think."

"Can you?" he asked slyly, playing with the buttons of her blouse.

Forcing herself to look up at him once more, despite her intense embarrassment, Toni was surprised to see that he was smiling broadly.

"Aren't you furious with me?" she asked.

"Why? For showing that you care about me? Toni, I am well aware how proud you are. You never would have given yourself away unless you were furious with me. Damn these buttons," he muttered, as his fingers fumbled with the tiny things. Finally, he forced them open and Toni felt her blouse part. In a moment, he had slipped it off her shoulders.

"But, Theo, I behaved so badly."

"Yes, you did. But don't worry, love, I'll give you a chance to make it all up to me."

"You're laughing at me," she finished helplessly.

As he undid the clasp of her sheer, lacy bra, he stopped and looked at her deeply. "I'm not laughing at you. I feel a great many things toward you right now, but amusement isn't one of them. I'm just plain relieved that you're no longer telling me to get the hell out of your life. I know how things must have looked to you and I don't blame you for being mad."

He finished removing the bra and Toni felt her bare breasts brush against his jacket. "But at the moment, I think we've talked enough. There's only one way, really, to show you how I feel about you."

He picked her up as easily as if she were a rag doll and carried her into the bedroom. While the storm raged outside, inside Theo and Toni let their profound desire for each other erase the memory of their own stormy interlude.

# 9

On a glorious October morning, when the sun shone brightly and the ocean was a glistening aquamarine, Theo and Toni drove up the coast highway to Santa Barbara. They were in Toni's convertible with the top down. The air had been cleared by the recent storm and for once there wasn't a line of smog along the horizon.

While Theo drove, Toni leaned back and let the wind toss her curls. Neither said very much. Occasionally they glanced at each other, smiling happily. But there was no need for conversation. A great many uncertainties had been swept away during their brief, but painful estrangement. Though they had always been deeply drawn to each other, now their attraction was made more stable by their knowledge of how much they meant to each other.

Toni felt happier than she could ever remember feeling. When she let herself think about the future, to the time when Theo would inevitably leave on another assignment in some distant part of the world, she grew somber. But she didn't want such nebulous worries to spoil her current happiness. So she forced herself to concentrate on the present.

*Now* is all that matters, she told herself. I'll just be thankful for what I have at this moment, and not worry about losing it. There will be time enough for sadness when he leaves.

Only one thing marred her perfect bliss. Theo showed his love for her in an infinite variety of ways, some tender, some passionate. But he would never actually say, "I love you." When she spoke those words to him, shyly yet with conviction, he responded affectionately, "You mean more than anything in the world to me."

Toni knew this was his way of avoiding an ultimate commitment, of opening himself up to her completely. Most of his barriers were down now with her. But some stubborn ones remained.

Trying to clear her mind of these vague but persistent worries, she looked out at the ocean. It lay smooth as glass under a clear, powder-blue sky. The mountains that sloped down to the pristine white beaches were brown now from a long summer without rain. Toni knew they would turn emerald-green in the winter when the short-lived Southern California rains finally came. She loved Malibu for its contrasts—the vast ocean, the smooth, white beaches, the rugged mountains of the Santa Monica Range. On a beautiful morning like this, with Theo beside her, she felt that this was the best place in the whole world to be.

She couldn't help reflecting that Theo was like this area, in the sense that he, too, was a mass of contrasts. He was sensitive yet cynical; tender yet brutally passionate. He was an enigma she knew she might never find the answer to; yet this only made him more irresistible to her.

As they grew closer to Santa Barbara, the landscape grew greener, more lush, the hills more gently rolling. Toni began to wonder seriously what Leonie would think of Theo. She wanted Leonie to like him, and thought that she probably would. Yet she couldn't help worrying about it because it meant so much to her that the two people she loved most should get along well. Toni was only too aware of how sharp-spoken Leonie could be when she disliked someone. Leonie had always spoken her mind frankly, and as she grew older she used the advantage of age to dispense with all polite convention at times. It was entirely possible that she might behave as she had with Robert. She had taken one long, critical look at him, then promptly dismissed him, refusing to acknowledge his presence ever again. Looking back on it now, Toni couldn't help grinning at the recollection. Robert was definitely not used to being treated as anything less than a V.I.P.

But if Leonie should take a dislike to Theo and behave in the same way, Toni didn't know what she would do. She wanted to simply say to Leonie, "I love this man so please be kind to him." But she couldn't do that. It would be up to Theo to fight his own battles with Leonie. Toni knew he wouldn't let her do that for him.

Stop worrying, she finally told herself sternly. She knew that Leonie was a terrific judge of character. Leonie would almost certainly see in Theo the same rare qualities that Toni did—*if* Theo would let her. The quality of being very much his own person, utterly without pretense, was so unlike Robert. It was a quality that Leonie shared. She had lived her life her way and encouraged Toni to do the same. In an odd way, Toni suspected that Leonie and Theo were more alike, more compatible, than she and Theo were. They were both, basically, free souls.

Just as they reached the suburbs of Santa Barbara, Toni directed Theo to turn off onto a side road. They drove for miles through the gentle foothills before passing through a massive wrought-iron gate. A single-lane paved road wound between towering sycamore trees to a huge old Spanish-style hacienda. Even though Toni had grown up here, she was always a bit awed by the house each time she returned. It was truly magnificent, a relic of a more gracious bygone era. The adobe tiles glistened a deep, coppery red in the sunlight. Huge flowering bushes of bougainvillea and azalea in a riot of red and purple climbed the walls. A veranda, lined on one side by open arches, extended along the entire front of the house. In the center, stone steps led up to the massive double oak doors.

Shooting Toni a surprised look, Theo said, "Somehow I wasn't expecting the Taj Mahal."

Toni laughed. "Leonie told me once she won it in a poker game. I half believe her."

"*This* is where you were raised?"

"Uh-huh. It was terrific for playing hide and seek. Once they couldn't find me for three hours. Leonie tanned my hide when she finally found me."

Theo stopped the car in front of the entrance. Beyond the curving drive, a fountain bubbled loudly in the silence of the countryside. Sunlight glinting in the cascading water formed a tiny rainbow.

Theo had barely turned off the engine when the doors to the house were flung open and a small woman dressed in flamboyant crimson silk slacks and tunic came out to greet them.

"Leonie!" Toni shouted happily. She jumped out of the car and ran to the woman, hugging her affectionately.

Theo got out more slowly, not wanting to interrupt the reunion. By the time he got to them, they were laughing and talking excitedly.

Leonie Vallis had been a stunning woman when she was young. Even now, when she was past seventy, she was striking, with marvelous high cheekbones and huge, ice-blue eyes. She wore no makeup. Her face had no wrinkles, but a softness that comes with age, instead of the sheen of sleek young skin. Her hair was more silver than blonde now and she wore it becomingly short.

There was something intrinsically youthful about her. Her entire demeanor was energetic, open and exuberant.

Finally, she turned her attention to Theo. Her shrewd blue eyes scrutinized him carefully, missing nothing. He found himself shifting uncomfortably on his feet. Toni was aware of Theo's tension. She walked back to him and took his hand, squeezing it reassuringly.

"You must be the young man I was supposed to meet last week," Leonie began bluntly.

Theo had apparently decided to meet her head on. "Right," he answered matter-of-factly.

He didn't flinch as she continued watching him carefully. Her expression was guarded and it was impossible to interpret her feelings. Toni held her breath. This appraisal was so important to her.

Shooting a glance at Toni, who was waiting with baited breath, Leonie continued, "Well, I must admit you look like the sort of man who's worth waiting for."

Then she grinned broadly. Taking Toni's hand, she led her into the house. She called back over her shoulder, "Come on."

The interior of the house was as stunning as the exterior. Leonie had furnished it with exquisite antiques, but she had been careful not to overdecorate. The wooden floors were polished to a high sheen and were bare save for occasional richly colored oriental carpets. There wasn't the clutter of knickknacks and mementoes that are often found in the homes of the elderly.

The large rooms opened onto each other through broad, arched doorways. And the tall windows let in a great deal of sunlight. It was a bright, happy, surprisingly comfortable house. Like its owner, it had a great deal of class.

In the living room, sofas and chairs embroidered in bright colors were arranged around a large fireplace that covered one entire wall. On a square, dark-wood table, bright with a bowl of golden chrysanthemums, sat a lacquered tray. It held coffee and tea and a crystal decanter of brandy.

As Toni and Theo sat down on a small loveseat, Leonie sat opposite them in a matching wing chair near the table.

"You two must be thirsty after the drive," Leonie said brightly. "Would you like some coffee?"

"Yes, please," Toni answered, unable to keep a nervous note out of her voice. Leonie was daunting, to say the least, and Toni wasn't sure how Theo would take her.

"What do you take in yours, Mr. Chakiris?" Leonie asked, as she poured the steaming black liquid into gold-rimmed, white porcelain cups.

"Please call me Theo. And I take my coffee black."

"How about just a drop of brandy, Theo?" Leonie asked. "I've never known a reporter or photographer who didn't care for a touch of something strong in his coffee."

"Leonie, you're my kind of woman," Theo responded, smiling comfortably.

Toni let out an audible sigh of relief. It was going to be all right.

After handing Toni and Theo their coffee, Leonie poured a cup of tea for herself. It was a greenish-black liquid that had an odd aroma.

"Leonie, how can you drink that stuff?" Toni asked ruefully.

"It's what keeps me going, child. By the way, lunch will be served on the patio. It's such a gorgeous day, I didn't want to miss one bit of it."

Toni smiled happily. Though Leonie wouldn't actually admit it, she clearly liked Theo. And when her grandmother liked someone, she could be utterly charming. For his part, Theo was clearly impressed with Leonie.

It's going to be a marvelous day, Toni thought cheerfully.

"What are we having for lunch?" Toni asked.

"How does crab cocktail, spinach salad and some

fresh fruit from the garden sound? I planned something light because I thought you might want to go riding this afternoon. Do you ride, Theo?"

"Not with a great deal of style. But I can stay up on most horses." He added lightly, "In my business, you have to be able to handle whatever type of transportation is available."

"Ah, how well I remember," Leonie responded, leaning back against the chair comfortably. "I've ridden camels in Saudi Arabia and elephants in India. Nasty, smelly things, camels. All in all, I prefer elephants."

"Toni's told me a little about your career. I know you've covered some fascinating stories."

"It hasn't been dull, that's true. I was widowed early, you see, and had to figure out some way to support myself and my child in the middle of a depression. I had a tenacious personality even then, and a friend suggested I might be good at ferreting out stories. I enjoyed it immensely from the very beginning. I tried everything, especially the things they insisted weren't 'proper' for a woman reporter. I decided right then that since we have so little time allotted to us, I'd best not waste any of it. I've tried to cram as much as possible into my relatively short span of years."

Turning her attention to Toni, Leonie concluded, "And I was very happy when Toni finally decided to stop hibernating in Beverly Hills and pursue a career."

*"Leonie,"* Toni objected halfheartedly, knowing full well that it was impossible to censor her grandmother.

"Well, it's true. I'm too old to bother with polite lies. You must admit your life's been much less boring lately. The royal wedding, for instance. That was quite a spectacle to cover."

"What did you think of it?" Theo asked slyly, with a quick glance at Toni.

"It was the best show in years. And absolutely free to

watch. The world isn't much given to acting out fairy tales
anymore, you know. International terrorists and assassi-
nations are more in the modern line. It was a nice change
to see such a pleasant, old-fashioned concept as love and
marriage being given center stage for a while."

"You think it was true love, then?" Theo asked
pointedly.

"Don't you?" Leonie asked, just as pointedly.

"No."

Leonie looked thoughtfully at Toni for a moment, then
returned her gaze to Theo. "You're much too young to
be so cynical, young man. Whatever the real truth of the
matter, Charles and Diana looked as if they are deeply in
love. And they both certainly have a deep respect for
marriage."

"They have to, considering their position, since divorce is out of the question," Theo replied frankly.

"Sometimes, believing in something is enough to
make it so. They *want* to love each other, they're willing
to open their hearts to each other; therefore, they're in
love. And it was tremendously reassuring to the rest of us
who want to believe that such a love is possible. Why on
earth do you feel it necessary to deflate other people's
romantic notions?" Leonie asked sharply, her clear blue
eyes watching him soberly.

She had turned the tables on him neatly. She had the
clever interviewer's knack of getting to the heart of a
subject, getting past a person's defenses.

Theo hesitated before finally admitting slowly, "You
have a point. I have no right to tell other people what
they should believe, even if I think they're unrealistic."

"You believe love is unrealistic?"

Toni wished fervently that Leonie would give up, stop
pursuing this awkward subject. But she knew her grandmother was like a terrier. Once she got hold of a line of
thought, she would pursue it until she made the other

person see things her way. Or, which was much more rare, until the other person had made her come round to their point of view.

Theo answered Leonie's question frankly. "The idea that love lasts forever, that two people will always be happy with each other, is unrealistic. At least, most of the time."

To Toni's surprise, Leonie grinned broadly. "Ah, I see. You're just afraid."

Theo was taken aback. "What?"

"Scared. Plain and simple. You know, I'm continually amazed at how little courage young people have nowadays. You're afraid to give in to love because someday you may be hurt. That's self-defeating, you know. When I was young, it didn't occur to us to worry about what might happen years down the line. We simply rushed in where angels fear to tread, I suppose. But we let things take their course, accepting that there were no guarantees about the future. Nowadays, people want lifetime guarantees of happiness, instead of accepting that it's up to them to make their happiness. Why not take love as it comes, and worry about the end when it happens? You may be surprised. It may last forever."

To Toni's intense relief, the maid appeared, announcing that lunch was served on the patio. The conversation had taken a decidedly uncomfortable turn and she was glad to see it end. She had expected Leonie to talk to Theo about her interesting experiences as a journalist. She hadn't expected her to argue with him about his romantic philosophy.

"I'll show you a bit of the house on our way out," Leonie said as they rose.

She took them through the drawing room into a library lined with bookshelves and a music room with a gleaming black grand piano. Then they passed through a huge dining room with a massive table that could seat fifty people. Finally, they passed through French doors onto a veranda. Crossing the veranda, they descended several steps to a small patio at the edge of a garden.

A glass-topped, black, wrought-iron table was set for lunch. But before sitting down, Leonie led Toni and Theo over to the edge of the garden. It sloped down to a small stream a hundred yards away. A brick path meandered through the lush foliage. Stone benches were placed at intervals along the path.

"It's taken me years to get this garden right," Leonie explained proudly to Theo. "Don't ask me to name all the flowers," she continued, smiling and spreading her hands to indicate the myriad varieties of colorful blooms. "I told my gardener I didn't want anything rigid or geometric. I wanted something wild and natural. And *colorful*. I wanted every color in the rainbow, and I've finally gotten it."

"It's beautiful," Theo said sincerely, gazing out at the floral paradise.

They returned to the table then and sat down on wrought-iron chairs covered with bright green print cushions. Leonie poured chilled white wine that sparkled in the clear crystal glasses in the bright sunshine.

As they began eating the cold, thick slices of crab, Leonie said, "You know, Theo, when Toni first told me about you, I thought your name sounded familiar. I know we haven't met before because I would have remembered you. But I'm *sure* I've heard your name before."

"It's in a lot of magazines and newspapers," Theo responded, biting into a chunk of crab. "Even the wire services use my photos sometimes."

"No, I'm not referring to photo credits. Have you ever been in Santa Barbara before?"

"I went to the Brooks Institute for a while about ten years ago," Theo said, referring to a famous photography school.

"That's it!" Leonie exclaimed, laying down her fork and smiling broadly. "You had a showing of your photographs there, didn't you? In fact, you won some sort of special award as most promising student, or something."

"Yes. But like I said, that was about ten years ago. I'm surprised you remember."

"If they had been bad pictures, I would have quickly forgotten them," Leonie answered bluntly. "But they were good. *Quite* good. They were all studies of people, if I remember correctly."

Theo nodded. He seemed reluctant to pursue the subject. Toni didn't understand why. She also didn't understand why, in all their conversations, he had never mentioned that he had begun as an artistic photographer. She had always simply assumed that he started out covering conflicts. Now, she looked at Theo interestedly. This was an entirely new area of his character that was being revealed to her for the first time.

"I didn't know you began as an artistic photographer," she finally commented, when it became clear that Theo wasn't going to say anything further on the subject.

"I didn't actually sell anything," he responded shortly. Then, realizing that he was going to have to explain himself, he finished, "I left the Institute to cover Viet Nam. I just never got back to artistic photography after that."

"A pity," Leonie commented, watching him shrewdly. "You have an unusual talent for it. And it would certainly be less dangerous than being a war-eater."

Toni gave Leonie a quizzical look.

"War-eater is a term used to refer to war photographers," Theo explained, smiling wryly. He was leaning back in his chair now, watching Leonie carefully.

For some reason, Toni got the feeling there was a battle of wills going on. Her impression was confirmed when Theo continued bluntly to Leonie, "Obviously, I like what I do or I wouldn't do it."

"That's not necessarily true," Leonie shot back firmly. "There are *many* reasons why we do things. For the money. To impress others." Then, her blue eyes narrowing speculatively, she finished, "Or, because we're afraid to try to do what we *really* want to do because we might fail."

For a moment the atmosphere was electric with something unsaid but deeply felt. Then the mood was broken as a servant came to clear away the dishes and bring dessert.

"Well, how about going for a ride after dessert," Toni suggested brightly, trying to dispel the lingering atmosphere of strain.

"Sure," Theo agreed mildly. "But I didn't bring any riding clothes."

"Oh, I've got some extra ones around here somewhere," Leonie said. "While Toni changes, I'll take you to find them."

Theo shot her a vaguely wary look but said nothing.

When they finished eating, Toni went up to her old bedroom to change into the riding clothes that she kept there. She suspected that the suggestion to go riding had been made to give Leonie some time alone with Theo. Well, she could do nothing about that, she realized ruefully. If Leonie wanted to talk to Theo privately, she would fine some way of doing it. Still, as she dressed in jodhpurs and boots, Toni couldn't help wondering what Leonie wanted to say to Theo.

Leonie led Theo to a guest bedroom in the east wing of the house. In the large closet that ran along one entire wall was an assortment of men's clothes in different sizes.

Catching Theo's amused look, Leonie said merrily, "I know, it looks like a used clothing store for men. It's just odds and ends left by various guests over the years. Somewhere in there is a pair of hiking boots that Ernest Hemingway left. I'm sure there must be something here in your size that's appropriate for riding."

She searched through the clothes quickly, coming up

eventually with a pair of faded Levis and a checkered, western-style shirt.

Holding them up to Theo, Leonie asked, "Do you think these will do?"

"I think so," he responded. "They look about my size." As he took the clothes from her, he added matter-of-factly, "Now, what is it you want to talk to me about alone?"

Leonie smiled. "I appreciate your coming directly to the point. It makes things so much easier. If you don't mind, I'll speak frankly."

"Do you ever speak any other way?" Theo asked drily.

Leonie laughed easily. "No. Actually, I don't. It wastes time, you see, being polite, considering the proprieties, and time is something I have precious little of." Breaking off, she paused while she sat down in a nearby chair. Then she began again firmly, "I'll come right to the point, as you did. There used to be an old-fashioned concept that was basically concerned with asking young men what their intentions were. It's gone out of style now, though I personally think it should be revived. It has a great deal in its favor, not the least of which is the fact that it forces a young man to think about what he's doing. Toni means everything to me; she is quite, quite precious. I saw her hurt once and don't intend to see that happen again. So I'm asking you now—what are your intentions toward my granddaughter?"

Theo hesitated. He wasn't, surprisingly, irritated by Leonie's question. After getting to know her, he could very easily understand her deep feelings toward Toni and her desire not to see Toni hurt. He decided to speak as frankly as Leonie was doing.

"I don't know what my *intentions* are, as you call them. I care about Toni very much and would never mean to hurt her."

"No, I don't believe you would. But you might very

well hurt her unintentionally by not being willing to give as much as she is giving."

Leonie stubbed out her cigarette in an ashtray on a nearby table. "I want to tell you about Toni, Theo. When she was very small, she lost her parents."

"I know that," Theo said, wondering what this was leading up to.

"Yes, but you don't know how she handled that tragedy. She was terrified, of course. I'll never forget how she looked the night she came here. Her face was tear-stained and her eyes were filled with an intense fear of the unknown. But even then, when she was so very young, she didn't give in to her fear. She fought it. She didn't let it destroy her. She looked like such a pathetic figure at first, that terrified little girl. But I quickly realized that she was anything but pathetic."

Leonie stood and walked over to a tall window that looked out onto the garden. Parting the lace curtains, she gazed out for a moment, before turning back to face Theo.

"My granddaughter is a remarkable young woman, Theo, because she has the courage to go after what she wants. She doesn't let the possibility of failure or pain stop her. She has so much love to give and she doesn't hold it back for fear of being taken advantage of."

Theo's expression was tense now. "Are you saying that I would hurt her by taking what she has to give and giving nothing in return?"

Her level gaze met his squarely, blue eyes meeting brown ones unflinchingly. "No. I'm not saying that at all. But what I *am* concerned about is the fact that she may have more love to give than you do. It was the same way with Robert Lawrence. She offered him her heart in all its innocence, and he abused her. Toni wasn't truly in love with Robert; she merely convinced herself that she was. Glamor was the name of that period of her life. Her fires were banked the entire five years of her marriage. But now, you've kindled a fire in her, a blaze strong enough to warm her for a lifetime. She loves you profoundly."

Smiling pensively, Leonie continued, "I'm an old wreck of a woman now, but believe me when I say I know what it is to love that deeply. Even when the person who inspires such love is gone, the warmth of the love endures. No matter what you do, even if you leave her, Toni will love you forever."

Feeling somehow embarrassed by Leonie's words, Theo responded coolly, "You sound like an armchair psychologist."

"I do think I've developed a healthy judgment of character over the years. It's one of the few advantages of growing older." Then she finished grimly, "It boils down to this—despite her unhappy marriage, Toni isn't afraid to love. I think you are. And in the end that could turn out to be a very painful situation for her."

"I see. Don't you think you might be giving me too much credit? It's possible that I don't mean that much to her."

"Don't exhibit false modesty, Theo," Leonie shot back quickly. "It doesn't suit you. You're a very attractive man. The moment I saw Toni's face today, I could tell how deeply she's been affected by you. You've touched her in a way that no man has ever done before. The way she looks at you, her very walk and manner of bearing are different with you. What Toni feels for you is very rare and precious. You're the other half of her heart. Without you she isn't complete. That's the sort of feeling that most people go through their entire lives never experiencing. It's a wonderful, magical thing. But if you don't feel it, or, worse, if you won't let yourself feel it, you'll hurt Toni terribly. I think she could survive even that hurt. But I wouldn't want her to have to go through it."

In all his years as a war photographer, with his reputation for raw, reckless courage, no one had ever accused Theo of being afraid. Now, Leonie was bluntly doing so. And what was amazing to him was his reluctance to tell her she was wrong. Somehow, the denial just wouldn't come.

Afraid to love, he thought, considering this new notion as if it were an unusual seashell he found while walking along the beach. For some reason, he also pondered his work. It had been years since he'd thought seriously about his early days as an artistic photographer. Remembering the dreams he'd had then, it almost seemed as if that happened to someone else in another lifetime. Afraid to love because he might be hurt . . . afraid to make a commitment to the work that fulfilled him because he might fail. . . . He shook his head angrily. This conversation had gone just about far enough.

"I understand your concern for Toni," he said curtly. "But my relationship with her is strictly between her and me."

Instead of taking offense, Leonie merely nodded silently. Crossing the room, she stopped just short of Theo. "The stable is at the northern end of the house," she explained, then left.

# 10

～～～～～～～～～

Theo and Toni rode for two hours along a trail that meandered through the low foothills. Occasionally, they could see the ocean in the distance, but for most of the time they were surrounded by green hills and low, lush vegetation. As the more experienced rider, Toni was astride a spirited mount, a palomino gelding. Theo was on an aging, but still sprightly, bay mare.

It had been a puzzling afternoon, Toni thought pensively. Theo said nothing about his time alone with Leonie. But Toni was convinced that something significant had passed between him and her grandmother. It frustrated her to think that she couldn't ask about it. It was clearly a private thing.

Theo was silent and thoughtful as they rode side by side. But when they stopped by a tree to rest in the welcoming shade, he was more proprietary than usual; he touched her lightly on the arm and along the side of her cheek, as if he were studying her carefully for the first time. He'd touched her much more intimately than this before, of course, yet somehow this feather-light caress ignited her as if they were in bed together. She found herself looking forward impatiently to returning home that night.

"Theo, is something wrong?" she asked.

"What?" he responded, coming out of his reverie. "No, nothing's wrong. I was just thinking."

"A penny for your thoughts," Toni said, grinning.

"They're not worth it," he answered drily.

"Theo—are you sorry we came? I know Leonie can be a bit daunting at times."

"Leonie's a fascinating character," he answered slowly. "Very sharp. And I'm glad I met her. It's been . . . interesting."

"Want to get down for a while?" Toni suggested, noticing that Theo looked tired.

"Yeah. I haven't ridden in quite awhile, and I'm sure I'll be feeling it tomorrow."

They dismounted and tied the horses to a tree limb. Sitting down on the grass under the tree, Theo leaned his back against the trunk while Toni positioned herself comfortably next to him. As she laid her head on his shoulder, he wrapped his arms around her protectively.

"Why didn't you ever mention that you began as an artistic photographer?" she asked, unable to contain her curiosity.

She felt his arms stiffen and wondered why such an innocent question should bother him so.

"The subject never came up," he finally answered abruptly. Then, dismissively, "I gave it up a long time ago, anyway."

"But when you took that picture of the little boy and me at Hyde Park, that wasn't a news shot," Toni insisted, unwilling to let the subject drop as Theo clearly wished.

"Yes, it was," he shot back sharply. "The fireworks show was all part of the wedding celebration. *Vogue* simply chose not to use that shot."

"What did you do with it?"

"I filed it, of course. I file all my shots."

His tone was openly irritable now, and Toni decided it was time to change the subject. Besides, she couldn't explain to Theo why she was so interested in the type of photography he did. If she told him the truth—that she wanted him to settle down to a more stable job that wouldn't take him away from her—he would almost certainly feel pressured. His whole life—the work he did, his personality—indicated that he was a free spirit who didn't intend to be tied down to anything or anyone.

Even to her.

In her daydreams, she considered giving up her career to follow him as he pursued his. Her feelings for him were stronger than her interest in her work. This was both surprising and dismaying to her, considering the battles she'd fought with Robert over her desire to have a career.

Lately, she found herself thinking more and more of ways she could bend her life to Theo's career. She could become a freelance journalist, she knew, which would allow her to travel with him. But that would mean concentrating on the wars he covered. The idea of constantly dealing with death wasn't appealing.

Leonie had long ago established a trust fund for her that was substantial enough to support her if she chose not to work at all. But Toni had tried doing nothing while married to Robert and had quickly grown bored.

*Hell,* she thought, frustrated. There simply was no easy answer to the conflict between her career and Theo's, as long as he continued to cover wars.

"What's wrong, Toni?" Theo asked, as she sighed deeply.

"Oh, nothing," she said softly. "I was just thinking about a problem at work." She was glad her back was turned toward him. She couldn't look him in the eye and lie convincingly. She finished, "We'd better be getting back. It's getting late."

Glancing up at the sun that was hovering near the horizon now, Theo agreed.

By the time they stabled the horses, then showered and changed, Leonie had drinks waiting for them in the sitting room. The conversation was easy yet purposefully impersonal. Leonie related amusing anecdotes about her exploits as a reporter in the days when it was an openly cutthroat business. Theo laughed appreciatively at the often outrageous stories that were cleverly told.

Though the atmosphere was relaxed and cordial, somehow Toni felt that something was left unsettled between Theo and Leonie. Realizing that neither was likely to talk to her about it, she reluctantly decided to put it out of her mind.

After a delicious gourmet dinner, Theo and Toni took their leave. Leonie came out onto the front steps with them, despite Toni's concerned protest that it was too cool outside for her.

"A little fresh air never killed anyone," Leonie insisted stubbornly. Then, hugging Toni warmly, she finished, "Take care, child. I love you."

"I love you, too," Toni answered before getting into the car with Theo.

As they drove down the long drive, Toni looked back and saw Leonie still standing on the front steps, watching them thoughtfully.

The drive back to Malibu was quiet. It turned cold when the sun went down, so Theo had put up the top before they left Leonie's house. In the warmth and darkness of the car, Toni leaned against Theo, her head on his shoulder, his arm around her comfortably. Both were lost in their own thoughts, and said little. Toni couldn't begin to guess what Theo was thinking. Her own thoughts were depressing.

For the first time she squarely faced what kind of man she had fallen in love with—a man who offered nothing more than the present. There was no future with Theo. Only the delicious ecstasies of the present. But whatever happens, she realized soberly, it was worth it. Whatever pain she would feel when he was gone would be worth the infinite pleasure of knowing him now.

She sighed, a soft, wistful sound. In response, he tightened his arm around her, squeezing her shoulder with his hand. The feel of his fingers through the thin fabric of her blouse aroused her, reminding her vividly of the many ways he touched her in their private moments. After only a few weeks, he knew her body better than Robert had in five years. He knew the secret places where a touch as light as a whisper could make her moan with pleasure.

Thinking about this in the darkness of the car made Toni's breath come faster. She moved closer to Theo, pressing her breasts against him seductively. Facing the fact that she would eventually lose him made her suddenly want him very badly. She wanted to experience as much as she could with him in whatever time they had left.

Her eagerness was communicated to him. Though he continued to stare at the road ahead and to steer the car firmly with his left hand, his right hand began caressing her, slowly at first, then more purposefully. The flame that only he could ignite began to grow within her as something raw and elemental was awakened. She sensed a similar response in Theo, an electrically charged awareness, as if a spark flew between them.

As his hand lightly traced the outline of her breasts through her blouse, then began undoing the buttons, she felt her breasts swell in response. She yearned to be free of the blouse and the sheer silk bra so that his hands could stroke her bare skin.

Looking up at Theo quickly, Toni saw that his eyes were glowing now with a sensual light.

Suddenly he reached under her loose blouse and unhooked the front of the bra, freeing her breasts. Immediately his hand pushed up the blouse. The rounded curves of her breasts rose and fell in anticipation and agitation. His hand roamed over her bare breasts freely, massaging the nipples that had already grown hard with desire. His fingers traced a sensuous circle around each nipple. Toni felt her body grow warm as a tropic tide seemed to flow through her.

As his fingertips continued a circular massage of her breasts, the warmth within her built. The movement seemed to grow more sensual with each passing moment. She felt a drugging warmth seep through her. The intoxicating effect was dragging her into an unknown region where she felt no inhibitions whatsoever.

At that moment, she wanted only to be naked in his arms, to feel his skin against her own. Unable to restrain herself, she began nuzzling his neck, licking and biting his earlobe, at the same time running one hand up his hard, sinewy thigh.

There was a hoarse intake of breath, then he muttered sharply, "Damn!"

She knew he wasn't angry at her but at the miles that still lay between them and her house where their mounting desire could be satiated.

Suddenly, he pulled over to the side of the road. The highway ran close to the beach here, almost on a level with it. It was a dark, deserted area of sand dunes and grassy knolls. Only occasional lights of passing cars indicated that anyone else existed in the entire world.

Theo turned off the engine, grabbed his jacket from the back seat, then took Toni's hand.

"Come on," he said tersely. With her bra still un-hooked and her breasts straining against her blouse, she followed him down to the beach.

The ocean lay like black glass under a sky dark save for a thin sliver of moon. In a hollow between two sand dunes, so hidden that even the lights of passing cars didn't penetrate, Theo threw down his jacket. Roughly, without caring if he ripped them, he tore off Toni's blouse and skirt. Her bra and panties followed.

Then he laid her down on his jacket. The brisk ocean breeze was a cold shock in comparison to the heat flowing within her. Looking into his dark eyes, lit now by a passion as overwhelming as her own, she knew that he wanted her as badly as she wanted him.

He lay down beside her, and his head dipped as his mouth explored her. She moaned, a low, guttural, animal sound, as his warm tongue found her rigid nipples. Her body arched to meet his. Impatiently, he tore open his shirt so that his skin could touch hers as he rolled over onto her. She could feel his heart pounding within his chest, could feel the soft, erotic tickles of the tiny, curling hairs on his chest as they brushed against her breasts.

She ached desperately for him now, not caring where they were or who might happen upon them.

His mouth came down on hers almost brutally, propelled by a ruthless, instinctive desire. His hands were rough now, yet she didn't mind the pain. She was filled with a white-hot desire now as she molded her body to his. Moving with sensuous abandon, she longed to be even closer to him, to be part of him.

He quickly shed his own clothes, and after only the briefest moments of unbearable suspense, Toni felt the fulfillment of union with him.

# 11

~~~~~~~~~~~~~~~~~~~

It was Christmas time and the traditional holiday decorations in the stores and on the houses were in odd contrast to typically sunny Southern California weather. Plastic snowmen beamed in the bright sunshine on front lawns, and Christmas trees were decorated with fake snow. Despite the clear, light-blue skies and persistent sun the temperature was cool. The crisp nip in the air gave a hint of what Christmas was supposed to be like. And the magic of the holiday transcended even the plastic of the decorations.

Toni wore a burgundy suede jacket and matching suede boots over white wool trousers. Her cheeks were pink from the brisk, cold wind. And her eyes were bright with excitement. Christmas was her favorite time of the year because it reminded her vividly of the time when her parents were still alive. Each year when she saw the strings of brightly colored lights going up, she was flooded with memories . . . shopping for the tree with her father while her mother baked cookies shaped like angels . . . her father holding her high up on his shoulders so she could put the shiny silver star on the very top

of the tree . . . lying in bed late on Christmas Eve,
listening to her parents laughing and moving around
mysterious objects in the living room . . . waking up in
the morning to a tree magically surrounded by presents.

And always the best, the most exciting present was
from Leonie, sent from whatever distant part of the world
she happened to be in at the time.

During her marriage to Robert, Toni took refuge in
these memories. Robert's sole interest in the holidays
was as a time for parties. To him, this was simply the
height of the social season, when he could hold a cup of
steaming eggnog and discourse to a fascinated group on
the meaninglessness, triteness and overweening com-
merciality of the holiday.

This year, the second Christmas since her divorce, Toni
was determined to celebrate the holiday as she remembered it with her parents. She dragged an amused, rather
cynical Theo out to look for a tree and cajoled him into
buying one of the largest on the lot.

"It will *never* fit," he warned her, as they carried it
through her front door.

When he turned out to be right, she simply cut off the
top to make it fit, then began covering it with the dozens
of ornaments she had bought in preparation.

As Toni covered the tree with wooden angels and shiny
balls of every color, Theo sat in a chair by the fireplace,
where a fire burned cheerfully. He was sipping a glass of
brandy, and he had a crooked grin as he watched her
struggle to put ornaments near the top of the tree. She
had shed her jacket and was wearing a white cowl-
necked sweater over the white slacks. Her hair curled
over the big, floppy neck of the sweater, its color vivid
against the soft white background.

As she strained on tiptoe to reach the highest branch,
Theo laughed softly, his brown eyes warm with affection.

"You're too short," he said, grinning.

"And you're an incurable cynic. Why don't you just

say 'bah, humbug,' and get it over with?" Toni responded, the laughter in her violet eyes softening the sharp words.

"I can see this project will get nowhere without a man's touch," Theo answered, loosening the collar of his blue shirt and pulling it away from his muscular neck.

Rising, he walked over to Toni. Instead of taking the ornament from her, he picked her up bodily. He held her up just high enough to put the ornament on the branch.

For a moment, Toni was filled with a flash of déjà vu, a sense of having done this very thing before. And then she remembered—her father held her in just the same way to put ornaments on the tree. She caught her breath, speechless for a moment with the remembrance of such innocent happiness.

The moment passed. As soon as the ornament was hanging from the branch, Theo pulled her down so that her face was level with his. Then, he kissed her deeply. And her childhood memories were replaced by newer, stronger sensations.

Theo was still holding her when the doorbell rang. Releasing her reluctantly, he whispered, "Later, love."

He returned to his drink by the fireplace, while Toni answered the door. She couldn't imagine who could be dropping by this late. Carol was out on a date, and none of Toni's other friends would come by without calling first.

Opening the door, Toni was amazed to see Charlie Bickham standing there, grinning broadly. At her stunned expression, he laughed and said, "I know, I'm the *last* person in the world you were expecting tonight."

At the sound of Charlie's voice, Theo turned and called out happily, "Charlie! What on earth are you doing here?"

"Looking for you, of course," Charlie responded, as Toni said warmly, "Please come in."

She took his coat and asked him what he would like to drink.

"Something hot. Coffee, if you've got it," he answered. "I wasn't expecting L.A. to be so cold. I hope I'm not interrupting anything."

"Of course not," Toni said sincerely. "I'll be back in a minute with some coffee."

As she disappeared into the kitchen, Charlie sat down by Theo. He explained, "I called your hotel and they said you were here." Glancing around the warmly inviting house and at Toni, barely visible through the open kitchen door, he finished, "I can see why you prefer this place to a hotel room."

Toni put cups and saucers, a sugar bowl and a jug of cream on a tray. Then she poured coffee into a porcelain pot decorated with a deep emerald-green design, and took it all into the living room.

"What do you take in it?" Toni asked politely.

"Nothing, thanks. Just black, the stronger, the better."

After pouring Charlie a cup, and a cup for herself, Toni settled back in the crook of Theo's arm.

Charlie eyed them both carefully for a long moment before saying, "When I saw you two in London I thought you made a pretty pair. You still do."

Toni blushed, but Theo responded casually, "What brings you to L.A., anyway?"

"I'm on my way down to El Salvador. Things are getting hot down there again." He eyed Theo quizzically. "I hear through the grapevine that you've turned down a couple of opportunities to go there yourself."

Surprised, Toni looked over at Theo. She wasn't aware he'd had offers to cover the war there. The fact that he'd apparently rejected the offers pleased her enormously. Yet it puzzled her, also.

Theo said simply, "It's not interesting enough down there yet." Then he continued, obviously trying to change the subject, "How long will you be here?"

"A couple of weeks. I've got to get my film crew and supplies together."

"Oh, good, I thought you might be leaving right away," Toni said happily. "If you've got awhile, why don't you come over for dinner? Any night that's convenient for you."

"Ah, a home-cooked dinner for a change. Sounds terrific." Then, drily, "Can we make it a *tête-à-tête* or do we have to include Theo?"

"I'm afraid Theo is part of the package," Toni laughed, throwing Theo a quick, sidelong glance.

"You better believe it," Theo added firmly. "I know you too well to leave you alone with a beautiful girl."

"Can't blame me for trying. I guess I missed my chance in London. I should have told Toni everything I know about you, then she would have gladly run off with me instead."

"Fat chance, old buddy."

"Oh, stop it, you two," Toni interrupted their playful bickering. She was rather pleased, actually, at the proprietary way Theo was treating her. He was normally so hung up on being free that he didn't show any commitment in front of others.

"Terrific place you've got here, Toni," Charlie continued, looking around appreciatively. Then, to Theo, "A man could get awfully comfortable here."

Theo merely smiled in response, refusing to rise to the bait.

Toni watched both of them. There was an undercurrent to their banter that only Charlie and Theo understood. Charlie was hinting at something that Theo refused to deal with openly. And he was watching Theo as if he was seeing something new in him. Toni wished fervently that she could be alone with Charlie sometime to ask him about Theo. As his oldest friend, he must know the answers to some questions that had been plaguing her for some time.

As if a passing fairy had decided to grant her wish, Theo said, glancing at his watch, "I'm supposed to make some calls tonight to set up a photo session tomorrow. Will you excuse me for just a minute? I'll use the phone in the bedroom, Toni."

"Take your time, Theo," Charlie responded amicably.

Looking from Charlie to Toni, Theo said, "Actually, I think I'll make those calls real fast. Toni, if this bear tries anything, just yell 'cut.' He's so used to being a director that he'll automatically stop what he's doing."

When Theo had gone into the bedroom, Toni said, "Would you like something to eat? I have some chocolate cake that I just baked yesterday."

"Now that sounds good. The food on the plane was rotten."

"Come on into the kitchen with me so we can talk while I get it ready."

Charlie followed her into the tiny kitchen, then leaned against a counter, his arms folded across his broad chest while Toni set out plates and took the cake out of the refrigerator.

"Have you known Theo long?" Toni asked, trying to sound casual.

"For years. We've even worked together a couple of times. He's someone I know I can count on in a tight spot. There aren't too many men I'd say that about."

Cutting generous slices of the cake for Charlie and Theo, and a smaller one for herself, Toni continued softly, "I've known him for four months now, but he's still like a stranger in many ways. He's a hard person to get to know."

"That's an understatement," Charlie agreed. "He isn't the sort to lay out his life story right off the bat." Then, as Toni was licking some chocolate icing from her finger, Charlie continued unexpectedly, "You love him very much, don't you?"

Taken by surprise, Toni didn't know how to respond. Charlie was clearly too perceptive to be satisfied by a polite lie. Finally, she answered, "Does it show that much?"

He nodded. His expression was serious now, no longer teasing. "It's not the sort of thing you can hide. You should see the way your eyes light up when you look at him. I'd give anything to have someone look at me that way."

Toni grinned ruefully. "Not too subtle, huh?"

"Nope." Then, Charlie continued slowly, "But what's amazing is that he looks at you in the same way." At Toni's startled look, Charlie hastened to explain, "What I meant is that I've never seen him so taken with anyone before. It just hasn't been his style."

"I know. A different city, a different girl," Toni remarked, repeating what Theo had once told her.

"Yeah. He wrote the book on being footloose and fancy free. From what I saw, there wasn't anyone he couldn't walk away from. But I don't see him walking away from you so easily."

"Oh, Charlie, he will walk away someday, though," Toni responded, her tone heartfelt. "It's just a question of when." Putting down the knife she'd used to cut the cake, and slumping against a counter, she finished, "Making a commitment isn't what he does best, is it?"

"Until now it hasn't been," Charlie agreed frankly.

"Why? I know how sensitive, warm and caring he can be. He feels things so much more than he lets on. Why does he keep up this façade of being hard and cynical?"

"That's a complicated question, Toni." Suddenly coming to a decision, Charlie continued firmly, "Listen, are you free for lunch tomorrow?"

"I should be."

"Let's get together. And I'll try to explain Theo Chakiris to you. Believe me, it's going to take awhile."

Toni smiled gratefully. "Okay. It's a date."

As she and Charlie returned to the living room, Theo came out of the bedroom.

"Sorry I took so long," he apologized. "I have to go through a Vietnamese interpreter and it gets complicated arranging things with him and then with the people I want to shoot."

"That's okay," Charlie said. "I used the time to try to persuade Toni to run away with me. But she seems to prefer a Malibu beach house to El Salvador slums. Can't imagine why."

Toni laughed indulgently. "Charlie, I'm just beginning to realize that you're *all* talk."

"Please," Charlie protested, "you're ruining my reputation. I'm a hot-shot director, remember? Don't you know I'm supposed to have lovely girls hanging all over me?"

"Oh? Where are they, then?" Theo asked drily.

"I'm sure they'll turn up as soon as they hear I'm in town."

Watching Charlie joking with Theo suddenly gave Toni an idea. He was a wonderful person, funny, sincere and nice. And more than a little attractive, she thought, if you like the cuddly, teddy-bear type. He'd be just right for Carol, she decided, making a mental note to ask Carol to come to dinner the same night that Charlie came.

# 12

Toni met Charlie the next day at the Cock 'n Bull Restaurant on Sunset Boulevard. The choice of restaurant was his, and it suited his personality. A wood-paneled building decorated with English photographs and mementos, it had been a gathering place for writers and other creative types for forty years.

Toni and Charlie were seated at a small table in a corner. When the waitress left after taking their order, Toni cocked her head to one side and began immediately, "So, tell me about Theodopolus Chakiris."

Charlie took a long sip of the beer the waitress had just brought, then leaned back in his chair. One hand rested on the table, while the other brushed through his unruly hair.

"Either you're a very direct lady, or you've got it bad," he teased.

"I'm afraid I've got it bad," Toni admitted.

"Like I said, Theo's a complicated person. He's a mass of contradictions in a lot of ways. You know, even in his war photos there's often an element of some softer emotion. I think the only way to explain him is to look at how he was raised. Once when we were in San Francisco together, I met his family. I learned a lot about his past then. His father was a Greek immigrant."

"I know. He told me."

"Did he tell you about his mother?"

"Only a little. He seemed reluctant to talk about her."

"I'm not surprised. He rarely talks about her, even to me. She died when he was eight. His oldest brother, Alex, told me a story that I think says a lot. On the way to the cemetery, their father, who was apparently a tough old bastard, told all the boys not to cry in public. He said they had to be men. Now, remember, he's talkin' to *boys*. Alex, the oldest, was only fourteen, I think. Anyway, during the graveside service, Theo started to cry. Not out loud or anything, just a tear or two running down his cheek. His father glared at him and Alex said if looks could kill, Theo would have been dead. Then the old man leaned down and told him in a loud whisper that women weep, not men. He ordered him to dry his tears. So, Theo wiped his cheeks and held back the other tears."

"Oh, how *awful*," Toni responded fervently, her heart aching for the frightened, unhappy little boy who wasn't even allowed to grieve for his own mother.

"Yeah. It's pretty sad. And what makes it worse is that apparently Theo was especially close to his mother. She liked to draw and he got his creative streak from her."

"So what he learned that day is that a man hides his emotions," Toni said slowly, pensively. This went a long way toward explaining Theo's reluctance to completely open up to her, to tell her he loved her.

"You got it. You were right when you said that Theo feels things deeply. He has more compassion than almost anyone I know. I've seen him take pictures of dead soldiers, then turn around and get blind drunk because he can't bear what he's seen."

The waitress placed dishes of salad in front of each of them, but Toni had no appetite. She watched idly as Charlie ate.

"I hate to sound like a shrink," Charlie continued between mouthfuls of salad, "but I think his mother's death affected Theo in another way, too. His standard joke is 'nothing good lasts forever.' Only I don't think it's a joke, really. I think that because his mother died when he was so young, he felt abandoned by her. And he can't quite get over the feeling that if he lets himself care about someone, that person will leave, too."

Toni thought about Charlie's perception. Remembering Theo's argument with Leonie—when he insisted that love is always bound to end at some point—Toni felt Charlie was right. Theo probably didn't feel he could count on anyone to always be there.

Well, there's no way I can fight that, Toni thought grimly. I can't guarantee Theo that I'll never die.

"Why does Theo cover wars?" Toni finally asked.

"Oh, for the same reasons most of us do, I guess. He's drawn to the drama of war. And he feels guilty because other guys are laying down their lives for something they believe in. Or, at least, for something their leaders tell them they should believe in."

Charlie's frank explanation matched Toni's own thoughts.

"To tell you the truth," Charlie continued slowly, putting down his fork and clasping his hands in front of him as he rested his elbows on the table, "I've been thinking of getting out of it. I've come close to getting nailed a couple of times lately, as has Theo. And it's beginning to occur to me that my luck might be running out."

"I wish you could make Theo see it that way," Toni commented ruefully.

Charlie eyed her carefully. "Who knows? He may be

coming to that viewpoint on his own. He's hung around L.A. a lot longer than this assignment requires. And like I said last night, I know he's turned down a couple of chances to go down to El Salvador. You've definitely had an effect on him, Toni."

"That may be true. But I still have the feeling I'm living on borrowed time with him, Charlie. I'm sure it's only a matter of time before he goes. Even when we're closest, when I've managed to pierce his armor a bit and reach the man inside, there's a wall between us. He's holding back. He still doesn't use the word 'love.' And we've never even discussed marriage at all."

"That's tough. When I saw you in London I thought, that's the kind of girl you marry, have kids with, fight with and make up with. I don't usually see Theo with that type. When I heard he was still seeing you, I couldn't believe it. You have no idea how unusual that is."

Toni grinned. "Thanks. I think."

Laughing, Charlie said, "That was meant as a compliment." Then, more seriously, "You're good for Theo. I just hope he realizes that."

"So do I," Toni agreed wistfully.

Back in the newsroom, Toni went into Carol's office. "What are you doing Friday night?" she asked without preamble.

"Um, let me think," Carol replied, leaning back and putting her feet up on her desk. "Ted went back to his wife and Alan is trying out the 'new celibacy.' So, I guess I'm not doing anything. Why?"

Toni smiled, shaking her head. "I don't know if you're kidding or serious."

"Unfortunately, I'm serious. My love life was more active in the sixth grade. What's up?"

"I'd like you to come over to dinner."

Carol eyed her sharply. "There's got to be more to it

than that. Since Theo turned up you've been spending
your evenings with him."

"So, maybe I've missed your company," Toni
countered.

"You see me every day. Come on, what's going on?"

"Okay. A friend of Theo's is in town. I asked him to
come to dinner, too."

"Ah, hah."

"Now, before you jump to conclusions, this really is an
innocent little get-together. I just thought it would be
more fun for Charlie if it was a foursome. You know, so
that he wouldn't feel like the odd man out."

"Charlie, huh? I suppose he's a really *nice* guy?" Carol
commented with a noticeable lack of enthusiasm.

"As a matter of fact, he is," Toni said forthrightly.
Then, firmly, "But before you turn down the whole idea,
think about it, okay? It might be an interesting change for
you to go out with someone who isn't a flake."

"Thanks."

"Don't mention it."

As Toni walked out, she stopped and said over her
shoulder, "Eight o'clock. Don't be late."

Carol grimaced at Toni's retreating back. But in spite of
herself, her interest was piqued.

Toni was putting the finishing touches to a prime rib
roast. She was wearing a cashmere sweater dress in a soft
shade of lavender. As she bent down to baste the roast,
she felt arms slip around her waist.

"I didn't hear you come in," she said happily as Theo
nuzzled her neck.

"Photographers have to learn how to be very quiet
sometimes. Some subjects, you know, have to be snuck
up on." Then, he finished, "I love that dress. The color's
*almost* as pretty as your eyes."

"Thank you. By the way, speaking of subjects, how's

the Vietnamese story coming?" Toni asked, keeping her face averted. She didn't want him to see that the question went beyond mild curiosity. She knew that after four months, Theo must be close to finishing the assignment. And that meant he would undoubtedly be leaving on another one.

"Oh, fine. It's basically finished. I'm just doing some final touches."

His tone was casual, revealing nothing of his feelings.

"Oh," Toni said softly. The steam from the open roasting pan floated up into her face. She told herself that was why tears were stinging her eyes.

Putting the lid back on, she straightened just as the doorbell rang.

"That's Charlie," Theo said, leaving the kitchen.

"Or Carol," Toni added. Then, seeing Theo's puzzled look, she admitted, "I asked her to come tonight, too."

Theo shot her an amused look. "A little blind date, huh. You missed your calling. You should have been a matchmaker."

I haven't shown much wisdom in the match I've made for myself, Toni thought soberly.

But as she watched Theo's retreating back, she said nothing. He was wearing a brown sweater and slacks. The snug-fitting sweater showed his well-muscled arms and shoulders. He was a heady mixture of physical strength and artistic sensitivity. The contrasting yet complimentary qualities affected her like strong wine, leaving her just a bit light-headed when she dwelled on them.

Standing in the door to the kitchen, she watched him unobserved. She realized that there was never a moment when she didn't desire him fiercely. He was every ideal she'd ever had about men.

And he was ultimately unattainable.

Opening the door, Theo said cordially, "Hi, Charlie, come on in."

"I brought some wine," Charlie explained unnecessarily, holding up a bottle of Montrachet.

Pulling herself together, Toni smiled and responded, "Great. It'll go perfectly with the cheese and fruit we're having for dessert."

"Something sure smells good," Charlie said, pausing by the kitchen door. "Roast beef?"

"Yes. I hope you like it."

"Are you kidding? I would like anything at this point that isn't served in a restaurant or on a plane."

Toni laughed. "What you need is a good woman to cook for you."

Theo gave her a wry glance which she tried to ignore.

"You may have a point. Know anyone who can cook and doesn't mind a husband who's gone ninety percent of the time?"

Laughing, Toni answered, "Well, no, actually." Then, trying to sound casual, she continued, "I've invited a friend to join us. She's my boss, Carol Bellini."

Charlie and Theo exchanged a look that was filled with meaning.

Responding to the look, Toni insisted with mock anger, "Now, listen, you two, this is a perfectly innocent get-together. And furthermore . . ."

Before she could finish, the doorbell rang again. Throwing the men one last irritated glance, Toni answered the door. Carol was waiting patiently, looking less than eager.

"Hi," Toni said brightly. "Come on in."

After taking Carol's coat, Toni introduced her to Charlie.

"Pleased to meet you," Carol said politely. The quick glance she gave Toni clearly meant, "He's not my type."

"Do you cook?" Charlie asked abruptly.

Surprised, Carol answered, "No. I prefer eating in restaurants. Why?"

Laughing, Charlie replied, "No reason." Then, looking at her appreciatively, he finished, "It isn't important anyway."

Theo led Carol and Charlie into the living room, while Toni went into the kitchen to put dressing on the avocado salad. As she worked, she caught snatches of the conversation. Charlie obviously found Carol very attractive, though she was much less taken with him.

"Dinner's ready," Toni announced, as she came into the dining room, carrying a tray with the salad.

The table was set with fresh flowers and candles. Carol complimented Toni on the lovely arrangement.

As Theo brushed past Toni, he whispered, "Not very subtle, but pretty."

Toni shot him a wry glance, before sitting down.

Throughout the meal, Charlie and Carol carried on a constant stream of conversation that quickly left out Toni and Theo. Toni didn't mind at all, while Theo was silently amused.

Charlie brought up every subject from sports to politics, and in each area he and Carol disagreed. It rapidly became clear that they had almost nothing in common, aside from a mutual interest in current events. Yet Toni wasn't dismayed. Carol had abandoned her reserved attitude and was talking animatedly with Charlie. Their disagreements were interspersed with jokes, and they were clearly enjoying arguing with each other.

When the meal was over, Charlie and Carol carried their wine glasses into the living room to continue a disagreement about politics. Theo helped Toni clear the table. As they took some dishes into the kitchen, he whispered, "Great going, cupid."

"Actually, it's working out pretty well," Toni insisted. "They can't take their eyes off each other."

"That's because they're too busy arguing about everything under the sun."

"They don't have to agree," Toni said firmly. "They

just have to enjoy each other's company. And, obviously, they do."

Flashing a dazzling smile that was warm with affection, Theo said, "Now *that* I can't argue with." And putting his arms around her, he kissed her deeply. As Toni pulled away from him reluctantly, he finished, "Let's get rid of those two and spend the rest of the evening alone."

"Mmm, that does sound appealing," Toni agreed, reaching up on tiptoe to put her arms around his neck and kiss him lightly. "But you know very well we can't do that."

"Why not?" he asked, nibbling her ear and pulling her close.

"Because," she responded breathlessly, "it would be rude."

"Rudeness never killed anyone," Theo teased, running his hands lightly up and down her back.

Toni pulled away while she still had the will to do so. "Take this," she ordered, putting a tray with wine, cheese and fruit on it into his hands. She finished, smiling, "And when they've gone, I'll remind you where we left off."

"I won't need a reminder," Theo responded as he left the kitchen.

When Toni joined the other three in the living room, Charlie complimented her effusively on the delicious dinner.

Thanking him, Toni said slyly, "You know, Carol's actually a terrific cook. Especially with Italian dishes."

"Oh?" Charlie asked, looking at Carol.

"But I would much rather do almost anything than bury myself in a kitchen," Carol responded drily, giving Toni a glance that clearly said, "Enough, already."

In a thinly disguised attempt to change the subject, Carol continued, "So, tell me about this El Salvador trip. When are you leaving, Charlie?"

"Next week," Charlie explained reluctantly. As he and Carol discussed the film he would be doing down there,

Theo listened avidly. He was showing a good deal more interest in the subject than he had done when Charlie first mentioned it.

Suddenly, as Toni sat next to Theo on the sofa, sipping wine and nibbling on a pear, she felt a vague sense of misgiving. Theo was asking Charlie specific questions about the trip. His questions were too pointed to reflect mere idle curiosity. Trying not to let her apprehensions get out of hand, Toni interrupted the conversation. "More fruit, anyone?"

"None for me, thanks," Charlie replied, patting his ample stomach. "I'm too full from that marvelous dinner."

"Maybe later," Theo said distractedly, sipping his wine thoughtfully.

Toni leaned back in a corner of the sofa and curled her feet under her. The pear she was eating was juicy and sweet, but her mind wasn't on the taste. She listened pensively as Theo and Charlie continued to talk about the trip.

"What day are you leaving?" Theo asked.

"Thursday. I've booked a flight for the whole film crew. Everything's set. This time next week I'll be in beautiful downtown San Salvador," he said drily. Turning to Toni, he finished, "When I think of you in this house on the beach I'll be jealous."

"Why go, then?" Toni asked, trying to make the question sound nonchalant.

Glancing at Carol, Charlie answered, "I've been asking myself the same question. I think after this I may hang 'em up, as they say, and stick to filming documentaries in this country. I've got an idea for a series on Appalachia that would be a lot safer than dodging bullets in Central America."

"You'll never quit, Charlie," Theo said confidently. "Chasing wars all over the world is in your blood."

"I used to think that," Charlie admitted. "But lately it's

occurred to me I'm not getting any younger. And if I ever want to have any stability, any permanence in my life I'd better start looking for it now."

Toni quickly looked at Theo to catch his reaction. He was watching Charlie with a disdainful expression.

"I'll believe that when it happens," Theo said, shaking his head.

"You're a confirmed cynic," Charlie answered.

Putting down her empty wine glass, Carol interrupted the disagreement. "I've got to be going, folks. Thanks for dinner, Toni."

"Do you have to leave so early?" Toni asked.

"Afraid so."

As she rose, Charlie rose also and said, "Let me walk you to your car."

"Okay," Carol agreed, smiling.

Toni and Theo both walked them to the door. Theo put one arm comfortably around Toni's waist, pulling her toward him.

"I'll be going, too," Charlie announced, helping Carol with her coat, then putting on his own.

"I'll give you a call tomorrow," Theo said to Charlie.

"Okay. If you don't catch me in, just leave a message," Charlie responded.

Toni stiffened at Theo's parting remark. She suspected that he wanted to talk to Charlie in private about the El Salvador trip.

As Theo shut the door, Toni returned to the sofa in the living room. Theo turned out the lights, leaving the room dark save for the light from the fire. The atmosphere was subdued, cozy. Shadows from the dancing flames played over the walls. Toni was sitting with her knees pulled up under her, her hands clasping her knees and her chin resting on them. She was watching the fire pensively.

Sitting down on the sofa, Theo said softly, "Come here."

She hesitated for a moment before joining him. Then

she nestled next to him, her head on his chest, his arm around her shoulder. They watched the fire in silence for a long time.

Finally, Theo spoke. "I think I'll go down to El Salvador."

Toni was expecting the announcement. Even though she had steeled herself for this moment, however, the pain was even more acute than she had expected.

"I see," she finally responded in a whisper.

"I won't be gone that long," Theo replied defensively.

But before he could say more, Toni interrupted in a firm voice, "No, don't explain anything." Then she reached up and kissed him deeply, with all the passion he had awakened in her on that long-ago night in London. Theo responded wholeheartedly, pulling her to him tightly as an electric shock arced between them.

Toni's mind was no longer on Theo's imminent departure. A more primitive, more powerful force replaced the awful pain she felt. Her body, on fire now, pressed against his. Her lips parted to let his tongue probe her mouth.

His hand roamed up beneath the soft cashmere of her dress to her slim thigh. She was like a glowing ember, ready to burst into flame. He kissed the curve of her throat, his lips moving inexorably down the deep V-neck of her dress.

"My love," she whispered, not even realizing she had spoken.

He shifted his weight, pulling back from her slightly. Then she felt him gently brush back the curling tendrils of hair on her temple. Looking up at him, she met his gaze. He was watching her, his dark eyes deep velvet, passion-dark. His finger traced the line of her jaw, before his lips lightly brushed the tip of her nose.

Toni ran her fingers lightly through his thick, dark hair, letting them come to rest gently at the back of his neck. "I love you," she whispered wistfully, fully conscious now of what she was saying. Her eyes searched his face for a response.

"You're everything to me," he finally said, his voice throbbing huskily as his lips remained only a hairbreadth from her own trembling ones. "But I don't want to talk about it. I want to show you how much you mean to me."

He undressed her quickly, expertly, then waited patiently while she undressed him. They lay together on the sofa in front of the flickering fire, their skin bathed in the golden glow of the flames. Toni ran her hands over Theo's back, glorying in the feel of his powerful muscles and smooth skin. He kissed her again and again, as if he couldn't get enough of her.

Toni felt her whole body reach out to him. Her lips sought his hungrily as she throbbed with a passion that obliterated everything else in its intensity. She was trembling now, not from cold but from the warmth seeping through her.

Finally, when she was breathless with desire, she pulled back, looking at Theo intently. She saw the familiar firm, wry mouth, the hard chin, the brown eyes so deep and compelling that she felt she could look into them forever and still not know everything about him.

"All those years," she whispered wonderingly, "I never knew it could be this way."

"It's supposed to be this way," Theo responded tenderly. "Anything less is . . . just not enough."

Then his probing tongue parted her soft lips. She let her tongue touch his, caressing it, curling around it, as her hands spread over his bare chest. His skin was warm to the touch, and she felt his muscles quiver as her fingers lightly roamed over them. The dark, softly curling hair on his chest brushed the tips of her fingers, making them tingle with delight.

His hand cupped her small, full breast as his other hand was entwined in her hair. One finger lightly stroked the tip of her breast, feeling it grow hard. His mouth explored her whole body now, traveling over the trembling pulse in her throat, her gently curving shoulder, her breast.

Toni moaned, a low, animal sound deep in her throat.

Theo's lips continued their erotic journey. His tongue lightly flicked the tips of her nipples and his teeth gently bit the heaving swell of her breast. Then his lips moved to her tiny waist and quivering stomach. Her hips arched against him, then instinctively began to move slowly, rhythmically, as his lips traveled further toward the tightly curling tendrils of red-gold hair.

Toni was beyond thinking now, beyond control. Her tightening muscles craved release.

As always, Theo was passionate yet tender, playing her with infinite patience, fanning the flame of her desire until she was begging for fulfillment.

When he could contain his own driving desire no longer, he took her ruthlessly.

Toni felt her breath mingle with his, her racing heartbeat match his, her skin meld with his, until they were one. . . .

Toni drifted back slowly from the sweet oblivion that she always felt at the end of making love with Theo. Looking at the nearly dead fire, she realized that she felt like one of the barely glowing embers that had earlier been blazing with a white heat. She was exquisitely satisfied, every fibre of her being relaxed in utter contentment.

Turning her gaze to Theo, she thought pensively, I am yours, body and soul. But do you really want me?

Theo rose and left the room, returning shortly with a soft plaid blanket. After covering Toni, he bent down to put more wood on the fire. His face was turned away from Toni's.

"Will you leave with Charlie on Thursday?" she asked slowly.

"Yeah. There's nothing to keep me here."

She died a little inside.

Realizing what he had said, Theo hurried to explain, turning to face her. "I mean, the assignment's over here. But I'll be back as soon as I'm through down there."

"How long will you be gone?"

"It's hard to say. But it shouldn't be too long." Then, nuzzling her ear, he finished huskily, "Even guerrillas couldn't keep me away from you too long."

His reassuring tone, the softness of his face brushing against hers, were almost too much to bear. She didn't want to be away from him, even for one night. All other considerations, everything else she wanted in her life, paled next to that one overwhelming fact. At that moment she admitted to herself what she had known since she first looked into his eyes during the fireworks display at Hyde Park. She would gladly give up everything to be with him.

"You know," she began, trying to make her tone sound casual and light, "I don't have to stay here. I could chuck my job, this house, everything, and be your camp follower."

"You mean, come down to El Salvador?" Theo asked, clearly surprised.

"Sure. I'd love to see what's happening down there firsthand."

She waited, holding her breath. Everything depended on his reaction to the offer she had made apparently so glibly.

"You'd hate it," he said flatly. "It's no place for a woman. They kill nuns down there, remember?"

It took all the courage she possessed not to cry then.

Fighting back the tears, she responded smoothly, "Sure, it was just a wild idea. I couldn't seriously consider giving up my job just when I'm beginning to get somewhere."

She closed her eyes, pressing the lids tightly against the bitter tears.

"There's some of that wine left that Charlie brought," she said. "Why don't I get some."

"Good idea."

"I'll just slip into a robe first. It's cold tonight."

In her bedroom, she put on a robe, then went into the bathroom and splashed water on her face. Looking at herself in the mirror, she saw a ravaged, hopeless expression. "You win some, you lose some," she told herself softly. But the dry humor of the words was belied by the hopelessness in her tone.

# 13

The Pan American terminal at Los Angeles International Airport was nearly deserted at midnight on Thursday. Most passengers had already boarded the flight to El Salvador, and only a few tired-looking travelers were waiting for other flights.

It was a rainy, windswept night. Through the glass walls of the concourse, Toni saw the rain covering the ground in huge puddles and streaming down the side of the plane. Charlie and Theo stood near the door leading to the jetway. Charlie carried one small bag, while Theo had two cases filled with cameras and other photographic equipment.

"Well, I'd better get on board," Charlie said. Leaning over to kiss Toni's cheek affectionately, he finished warmly, "Take care of yourself."

"I was going to give you that advice," Toni responded with equal warmth. "Bye, Charlie."

"Tell that boss of yours that I'm going to call her the minute I get back," he finished, grinning.

"I will," Toni answered, as he waved once, briefly, then passed through the door.

Toni turned hesitantly to Theo. This was the moment she had dreaded all week, the moment when she would have to put on the greatest act of her life.

Pretend it's all right, she kept telling herself all evening. Pretend your heart isn't breaking.

"Well, you'd better be going, too, or they'll leave without you," she said casually, smiling up at Theo.

He looked down at her, a mixture of longing and hesitation in his eyes. For one brief, glorious moment, she thought he might change his mind, might decide to stay with her.

Then he shattered her fragile hopes when he smiled tenderly and said, "Right."

He kissed her deeply, demandingly, stirring her body and soul as profoundly as he had the first time he touched her. It was a bitter reminder of the long, lonely nights she must now face. Breaking off abruptly, he whispered, "I'll be back, love," then hurried through the doorway and down the jetway.

Toni stood rooted to the spot, her violet eyes swimming with the tears she could no longer hold back, her lips trembling. Then, whirling around furiously, she ran away from the boarding area, away from the plane whose engines were beginning to roar, away from the place where she had said good-bye to the man she loved beyond all hope and reason.

As she drove away from the airport on that dark, rainy December night, Toni wiped her eyes, sniffed once or twice then straightened her shoulders.

Thinking through the situation, she told herself bleakly, You lost again, girl. You lost when you offered to go with him and he rejected you, and you lost tonight.

But crying, she realized, was useless. It wouldn't bring Theo back. He would always do exactly as he pleased, not allowing her love for him to tie him down in any way.

Well, I'm not going to spend my life driving home from airports to cry alone in an empty bed, Toni vowed. I'll never cry for Theodopolus Chakiris again, she told herself firmly, her hands gripping the steering wheel purposefully as she headed into the stormy night.

# 14

~~~~~~~~~~~~~~~

Carol stopped by Toni's desk, dropping an assignment sheet on top of a pile of papers. Toni was timing a story that was due in just minutes.

"Just a sec," Toni said without looking up. She continued listening to the tape recording for nearly a minute, watching a stopwatch carefully. The moment the recording ended, she pushed the stop button on the watch. Scrawling some numbers on the side of the typewritten story to indicate its length, she handed it to a passing reporter.

"Jeff, can you give this to Stan?" she asked.

"Sure," he said, taking it and continuing on his way.

Taking a deep breath, Toni leaned back in her chair. "What can I do for you?" she asked Carol tiredly.

"For one thing, you can stop driving yourself so hard," Carol began firmly.

"I'm just doing my job, boss," Toni responded with an undertone of self-mockery.

"Your job doesn't include staying here late every night and coming in on weekends."

"I don't have anything better to do with my time."

Carol frowned, then said softly, "You can drive yourself till you drop and it won't do do any good. I know. I've tried that myself. How do you think I got so far, so fast, in this cutthroat business? I was motivated by a hell of a lot of frustration and rejection."

Toni said nothing, but the exhaustion and unhappiness in her eyes was painfully apparent.

"Have you heard from him?" Carol asked.

Toni didn't have to ask who Carol meant. She shook her head negatively. "Not since last week when he called. He said they were going out into the countryside, and he probably wouldn't get a chance to call again until they got back to San Salvador."

"You need a break," Carol insisted. "Join me for a cup of coffee in the commissary."

"I've got a ton of work to do," Toni began.

But Carol interrupted her. "I'm your boss, remember? I'm ordering you to have a story conference with me in the commissary right now."

"Okay," Toni smiled halfheartedly.

They sat at a small table in a corner. After taking a short sip of coffee and grimacing at the awful taste, Carol said conspiratorially, "I have some news but you've got to keep it under your hat."

Smiling, Toni asked, "Office gossip? Don't tell me Jim is finally leaving his wife for Lorene?"

Carol grinned good-naturedly. "Don't be ridiculous. I wouldn't be acting so secretive about Jim's well-known love life. Everyone, including his wife, knows what he's doing. This is serious stuff, kiddo. The network's going to add a woman co-anchor to their morning news show. And you're one of the people being considered."

Whatever Toni had been expecting, it wasn't this. "Are you kidding?" she asked, even though she knew that one thing Carol didn't joke about was career advancement.

She was too ambitious herself, and had encouraged Toni to be the same way.

"I just talked to a guy I used to date at the network. He's part of the decision-making group. He asked me if I would like to join their staff of producers, if they choose you. Needless to say, I said yes. He made me swear not to tell you, but I kept my fingers crossed so the oath didn't count."

Toni laughed at Carol's childlike duplicity. "I just can't believe it."

"Well, you'd better believe it, girl, because you could be spending New Year's Eve in New York."

"That soon? But that's only two weeks away."

"I know. They don't waste time when they decide to do something."

"But why me?"

"Oh, come on, Toni, don't get modest. I told you that you did a terrific job covering the wedding in London. The network honchos were apparently *very* impressed with that. You're a good reporter, and the fact that you're attractive is icing on the cake." She finished, musingly, "I can see it now . . . dinner at Elaine's, ice skating at Rockefeller Center, weekends in lavishly refurbished Connecticut farmhouses."

"Carol, they haven't made the decision yet," Toni interrupted.

"Oh, don't be so cynical. You've been around Theo Chakiris too much."

I haven't been around him nearly as much as I would like to be, Toni thought ruefully. Forcing him from her thoughts, she asked, "When are they going to make a decision?"

"In the next few days. They're looking at film of all the women they're considering. I sent over that piece you did in London comparing that shop girl's wedding to the Princess of Wales'. They'll *love* it. You were witty and warm, and that's what they're looking for."

Suddenly Carol stopped and looked at Toni carefully. "You know, I expected you to be bouncing off the ceiling when I told you. Instead you look less than enthusiastic."

Toni grinned ruefully. "It isn't definite yet. I don't want to get my hopes up, that's all."

"No, it's more than caution," Carol insisted. "It's Theo, isn't it? You don't want to leave him."

"Carol, in case you haven't noticed, *he* left me."

"He'll be back."

"Sure. But for how long?" Toni sighed deeply.

"Hey, buck up, kiddo," Carol said brightly. "I know how much you miss him, but you *do* have other things in your life. And those other things are beginning to look pretty good."

"I know. Thanks for telling me about this. I appreciate it. I *really* do."

Though she tried to inject some enthusiasm into her voice, the bitter truth was that the job in New York didn't mean nearly as much to her as Theo did.

Toni spent Christmas Eve in Santa Barbara with Leonie. Leonie tried to make it an especially festive occasion, with a huge, gaily decorated tree and lots of outrageously expensive presents. But a white mink cape and a diamond-and-ruby watch couldn't dispel Toni's air of sadness.

Finally, after a quiet dinner, Leonie said firmly, "He'll be back, you know. He cares about you a great deal. More than he realizes, perhaps."

"I know he'll be back. And I suspect he cares for me as much as I care for him. But he doesn't want to admit it. He won't even say, 'I love you.'"

"Oh, he loves you all right. You may doubt it at the

moment, child, but the truth is, the man's smitten. I know his type well. They don't stay around this long unless they're well and truly hooked."

"Well, it would be nice if he could admit it."

"That's another thing altogether. He probably doesn't say the words because they mean too much to him. They imply a commitment that he's afraid to make."

"The way things are going, I wouldn't be surprised if he spends the rest of his life running away from that commitment."

Leonie was silent for a long moment. She watched Toni shrewdly, catching the familiar signals that indicated her granddaughter was in the throes of a difficult decision. Finally, Leonie said slowly, "You're trying to decide what to do about him, aren't you?"

Toni sighed heavily. "Well, I don't intend to spend the rest of my life in this awful state of insecurity. I don't know where I am half the time. I seem to always be daydreaming about Theo. Even when I'm engrossed in something else, my work or a really good movie, he'll suddenly pop into my head. It's like trying to shake your own shadow."

She smiled then, through the tears in her eyes, as she remembered her firm resolve not to cry over him again.

Leonie laughed. "That's love, dear. It's awful, really, though God knows life would be dreary without it."

"Oh, Leonie, when my marriage ended, the worst part of it wasn't the realization that I'd wasted five years. I could accept that. I told myself it was a 'learning experience.' The worst part was thinking that there was no such thing as love, really. I mean, a love that lasts forever, an old-fashioned, romantic ideal. I thought I'd lost my basic idealism because of my experience with Robert. And that was the greatest loss of all. Then I met Theo. And suddenly, when I least expected it, and certainly didn't want it, I discovered that a love that transcends everything else can exist. The problem is to keep it from slipping away."

Her expression was so similar to what it had been when she was a young girl railing against the unfairness of life, that Leonie couldn't help smiling tenderly. "No one ever said life is fair," she said softly.

Toni looked up at her, then grinned sheepishly. It was a private joke between them, a line she had heard often from Leonie. Then the smile faded and she responded with heartfelt honesty. "Oh, but I want him so, Leonie."

"I know, Toni. Believe it or not, child, the fact that I'm very old now doesn't mean that I wasn't young and in love once. I *do* understand how you feel. I know how utterly wretched it is to want to hold onto someone who only wants to be free. But who knows—you may get what you want."

Toni shook her head. "No, I don't see that happening." Then, pulling herself out of her despondent reverie, she said, "Enough talk of Theo Chakiris. He isn't even here, yet somehow he's dominating my Christmas anyway." Showing a flash of her old temper, she finished, "I hope he's in the middle of some Salvadoran jungle, cold and wet and miserable."

Laughing, Leonie responded, "No, you don't."

"You're right," Toni admitted dolefully. "I hope he's thinking of me. And missing me as much as I miss him."

Her violet eyes misted with tears and it took a determined effort to hold them back.

The next morning, after a Christmas brunch of sparkling champagne and delicious, fresh-from-the-oven croissants, Toni returned to Malibu.

She spent the day catching up on some work she had brought home from the office. By the time the sun set, she was looking forward to a quiet evening with a good book. But as she sat on the sofa in front of a cheerfully burning fire, she couldn't concentrate on the words on the pages. Her mind kept wandering, thinking of Theo and what he might be doing at that moment. She remembered the night they made love on this sofa with such abandon, such delicious ecstasy. . . .

Her thoughts were interrupted by a knock at the door. Surprised, she wondered who could be coming so late on Christmas night. Carol, she knew, was visiting relatives in Ventura.

When she opened the door, she didn't recognize him at first. His hair was rumpled, his face was covered by several days' growth of beard and his clothes were filthy and wrinkled. His eyes, reflecting utter exhaustion, were barely open. It was only when he spoke that she realized who it was.

"Merry Christmas, love."

"Oh, Theo!" Toni gasped, then flung herself into his arms.

He was nearly dead on his feet but he held her tightly as if he would never let her go.

# 15

~~~~~~~~~~

The day after Christmas was Saturday and Toni didn't have to go to work. She left Theo sleeping soundly and went into the bathroom where she changed into jeans and a bulky forest-green sweater. On her way back through the bedroom, she stopped to look down at him lovingly. He was sprawled on his stomach in the middle of the bed, one arm lying across the sheet where only moments earlier Toni had been lying. He was still dirty and unshaven. Last night he'd had barely enough energy to fall into bed after briefly explaining to Toni why he'd come back so unexpectedly.

Charlie had been wounded in a surprise attack by guerrillas while his film crew was working in a small village. And Theo had accompanied him back to a hospital in L.A. He hadn't slept, washed or changed clothes in the two days since Charlie was first hit.

After assuring Toni that Charlie's wound was serious but not critical, he fell immediately into an exhausted slumber.

Toni went into the living room, carefully closing the bedroom door behind her. She wanted to let Theo sleep as long as possible. After straightening up the house, she brewed some coffee and squeezed some fresh orange juice. She put the coffee and juice on a small lacquer tray and carried it outside onto the patio. It was cool but clear and sunny this morning. For a long while, she sipped the hot coffee and simply looked out at the ocean, a glistening azure blue.

"Good morning."

Toni turned and smiled warmly at Theo who was standing in the doorway. "Good morning, yourself, sleepyhead."

He looked much more like his old self this morning. He had showered, shaved and changed into a clean pair of slacks and a white, ribbed-knit sweater that contrasted appealingly with his olive complexion and dark hair.

Walking over to Toni, he bent down and kissed her deeply. Then he said huskily, "I think I forgot to do that last night. If this coffee didn't look so irrisistible right now, I'd take you back to bed, and *not* to sleep," he teased, sitting next to her.

She poured him a cup and watched as he drank it thirstily.

"How about breakfast?"

"Later. I'll take you down to that deli on the highway," he offered.

"That sounds great. But, Theo, are you sure Charlie's okay? All you said last night is that he's expected to recover."

"I didn't mean to make it sound that bad," he responded, wrapping his hands around the warm cup of coffee and putting his feet up on a chair. "The wound is serious. Without proper treatment there could be a permanent problem. That's why I insisted on bringing him back to L.A. instead of letting him be treated in a hospital in El Salvador. But he should recover completely. In fact, the doctor said he could be out of the hospital in two weeks."

"Oh, *good.*" Toni breathed a big sigh of relief. "I'd like to see him today, if he's up to having visitors."

"He'd love that. I'll call him later and we'll set up a time."

"Theo . . . what happened down there?"

"The usual thing," he answered grimly. "People trying to kill each other. We got in the way and Charlie didn't duck fast enough."

Only a few yards away, a seagull squawked and a pelican dove for fish. But Toni wasn't paying attention to these rituals of beach life. She was thinking that it could have been Theo who didn't duck fast enough.

Theo put down his coffee and reached out, taking Toni's hand, holding it securely in his own. Clearly sensing what was bothering her, he said gently, "I'm all right. It's *over.* There's nothing to worry about now."

Until the next time, Toni thought soberly.

Releasing her hand, Theo cupped her face in both his hands, forcing her to look at him closely. "All the way home, on the jeep from the village into San Salvador, and on the plane from there to L.A., all I could think of was *you.* Knowing I would see you soon . . . *touch* you . . . made the whole nightmare bearable."

She looked deep into his chocolate brown eyes and, as usual, her heart melted. She whispered helplessly, "It's just that I love you so very much."

"I know, love," he responded and pulled her close into the safe harbor of his arms.

At the hospital, Charlie was sitting up in bed, joking with the nurses as they came in and out of his room.

"I could make you a star," he said effusively to a pretty blonde nurse who came in with some medicine for him.

"I thought you made documentaries," she responded, grinning good-naturedly.

"Well, yeah, but listen, even the biggest stars had to start *somewhere.*"

She left, giggling and shaking her head.

"And to think I was worried about you," Toni said drily.

"I'm invincible," Charlie boasted. But the boast was cut short by a spasm of pain that contorted his face, wiping the grin from it.

"Are you okay?" Toni asked quickly. "Shall I call the nurse?"

"I'd like an excuse to see her again," Charlie said, recovering his humor as the spasm passed. "But I think she's getting suspicious. I've called her in here four times today."

"Well, if you're sure . . ." Toni responded hesitantly.

"Seriously, I'm okay," Charlie insisted. "It's Theo you should be worried about. He's downright reckless. You should have seen the way he ran out in the middle of the gunfire to get me when I was hit."

Looking embarrassed and uncomfortable, Theo said curtly, "Forget it." Then, clearly trying to change the subject, he went on, "Just stop chasing nurses and concentrate on getting well."

Watching Charlie bravely hiding the pain, Toni realized once more what a terrific person he was. The girl who gets him will be lucky, she thought.

As if on cue, suddenly the door opened and Carol came in. Toni could tell that she was nervous, but was trying to hide it behind her usual bravado.

"You know, Charlie, the last time I saw you you didn't tell me our next date would be in a hospital room."

Charlie was smiling broadly, clearly immensely happy to see her. "How on earth did you know I was here?" he asked.

"Theo called me," she explained. Then, looking at the flowers that covered the room, she went on, "I brought something I think you'll like better than carnations." And she pulled a six-pack of beer out of the large bag she was carrying.

Beaming, Charlie responded, "All right! So who cares if you can cook or not. You know what a man needs when he's really down."

Seeing the way Charlie and Carol were smiling intently at each other, Toni decided it was time for her and Theo to leave.

"We'd better be going," she said, nudging Theo.

"Right," Theo agreed. "See you later, Charlie."

As they left, Carol was sitting down on the edge of Charlie's bed, opening up a beer for him and gazing at him adoringly.

Toni was quiet on the ride back to her house. When they walked inside, Theo asked her if she would like a drink.

"No, thanks," she answered distractedly.

"Charlie really is going to be all right," Theo insisted.

"Oh, I know," Toni answered.

"Then what's bothering you?"

"I was thinking about what he said—how you risked your life for him."

"It wasn't that dangerous. Look, *he* was the one who got hit, not me."

"But it could have been you. I keep picturing it in my mind, you being hit, perhaps killed. . . ."

"Stop it!" Theo said angrily. Then, he continued more gently, "Don't dwell on it. It's *over*. All that matters is that I'm here."

He took her in his arms and held her tightly. But for once she didn't respond. Unlike him, she couldn't brush off what had happened. It made her feel sick inside, thinking about what might have been.

Later, when they made love for the first time in weeks, Toni felt driven by a relentless passion. It was as if she couldn't get enough of Theo, couldn't get close enough to him. She was convinced she'd come close to losing him forever. And even though he was here now, she knew he would leave again. And again.

# 16

On Monday morning, Toni was called into the office of the executive producer, Ben Sayers. When she got to his large, wood-paneled office, she found both Ben and Carol waiting for her. Carol was glowing and Toni immediately guessed what the meeting was about.

"I just got a call from the network," Ben began, getting right to the point. "A couple of weeks ago they started looking for a woman reporter to co-anchor the morning news show. To make a long story short, they've picked you. And they want Carol to go along as a producer."

Carol was grinning openly now.

Toni's first thought was that she had wanted this very badly since first going to work as a reporter. It was a rare opportunity, one any reporter would die for.

I should be ecstatic, she told herself.

Though she felt a surge of pride, the overwhelming joy she had expected just wasn't there. And she knew why.

"I know you must be very surprised and very happy," Ben continued. "And, of course, I'm happy for you, though frankly I'll be sorry to lose you both."

"I'll be sorry to leave, Ben," Toni finally said, meaning

it. "You gave me my first chance. And I'll always be grateful."

"I knew you could do it," he said simply. "I just didn't realize you'd do it so fast."

"Oh, for God's sake, Ben, don't look so unhappy," Carol finally said happily. "You're not losing a reporter and a producer. You're gaining a reputation for having groomed the newest star of network news."

Smiling, Ben responded, "I know. And, believe me, that's the only thing I like about this. Well, congratulations, ladies."

"Thanks, Ben," Toni said, taking his outstretched hand and squeezing it briefly.

"Now, I imagine you two have a lot to talk about, so why don't you take off for a long lunch."

"Thanks," Carol said. "We'll try to come back sober."

They were barely out the door when Carol gave a hoot of sheer happiness. "I *told* you," she said, her face lit by excitement, "New Year's Eve in the Big Apple!"

Though Toni tried to celebrate with as much exuberance as Carol clearly felt, she couldn't quite manage it. Her mind was on something entirely different from New York and the glamor and excitement of a network co-anchor job. The moment Ben confirmed that she had the job, she came to a decision regarding Theo.

When Toni got home that evening, Theo was in the shower.

"I decided to go for a swim," he shouted from the open bathroom door into the bedroom, where Toni was changing. As she slipped out of her dress and into more comfortable slacks and sweater, he continued, "What a mistake. The sun was shining but the water was *freezing.*"

When Toni didn't respond, he came out, toweling himself dry with a huge yellow velvet bathsheet. Seeing him standing there, naked, his hair curling damply over his forehead, and his dark-skinned body glistening wetly, made the thought of leaving him even harder to bear. The virile ruggedness of his body, his essential masculinity, was nearly irrisistible.

"What's wrong, hon?" he asked as she stood there awkwardly.

"Nothing. Actually, something terrific happened," she replied, trying to sound excited. "I've been offered a co-anchor job with the network."

"That's quite a promotion," he said, smiling.

"Yes. Of course, it means moving to New York."

He was jolted by this announcement. It hadn't immediately occurred to him that a network job would entail moving to the network headquarters in New York.

"I see," he responded slowly.

Toni waited breathlessly. So much depended on how he reacted to her leaving.

He was silent for a long moment. He stood utterly still, holding his towel loosely. Finally, he moved, picking up the clothes that lay across the bed and putting them on quickly. When he was dressed, he turned to face her and smiled wryly. "It's ironic, isn't it? Now, *you're* the one who's leaving. Somehow I didn't expect it." His expression was chagrined. Then he finished hopefully, "But New York is hardly the end of the world. I'm there at least as much as I'm in L.A. We can still see each other."

So, it's business as usual, Toni thought dejectedly. He doesn't intend to let this change have any real impact on our relationship.

"Tell you what," Theo went on brightly. "We'll celebrate. I'll take you to Perino's. Tonight you deserve to eat in the most expensive restaurant in town."

"Great," Toni managed to say, forcing a smile. But inside she was in turmoil.

All week, as Toni packed and made the myriad preparations necessary for such a major move, she waited for Theo to say something more. She was disquieted by the fact that, while Theo was concerned about her leaving, he wouldn't make a commitment to her. Every time they made love, Toni willed him to speak, to admit he loved her and wanted to be with her. In her happiest fantasy, he took her in his arms and said, "Let's get married. We'll work out where we live, our careers, somehow."

Then the last morning came, and she knew it was now or never.

Theo drove her to the airport, along with the few bags of luggage she was taking with her. Everything else was being sent on in a moving van.

After a skycap had ticketed her luggage, Toni went into the United terminal, followed closely by Theo.

"Seems like only yesterday you were here seeing me off," Theo commented.

"Yes, doesn't it," Toni replied absently.

At the gate, the agent exchanged her ticket for a boarding pass and said politely, "We've already started boarding, miss."

"Thank you," Toni responded politely. As she turned away, Theo took her arm and walked close beside her to the door leading to the jetway.

At the door, they stood silently, neither saying aything for long seconds. Finally, Toni looked up at Theo and whispered hoarsely, "I'd better be going." Then, before he could respond, she took his face in her hands, looked deep into his eyes, and said, "I love you."

He held her close and whispered, "I'll see you soon in New York. Nothing has changed, love."

"No," Toni said softly, but with an undertone of finality. Then, looking up at Theo, she finished, *"Everything* has changed, Theo. I won't be seeing you in New York."

Until she actually said the words, she wasn't sure she would be able to go through with it. Now, the hardest part was over. All that was left was picking up the pieces of her shattered heart.

"What do you mean? I'll be in New York a lot . . ."

"I know," Toni interrupted. Unable to look at him any longer, she turned away. "But I don't want to see you anymore, Theo."

He didn't respond at first. Finally, and obviously with great effort, he asked calmly, "Why don't you want to see me?"

"Because things will be exactly the same way as they are now. You'll fly in and out of my life when it suits your fancy. I'll never know when you're going to be in danger . . ." She stopped, angry now. "Oh, Theo, I could go on talking all day and it wouldn't do any good. What I want is commitment and you're not willing to offer that."

"I've given up every other woman in my life," he said tightly, his mouth set in a stubborn line and his eyes veiled. "I've told you how much I care about you."

"But you've never said 'I love you.' And you never will."

"You want a hell of a lot, Toni!" he shot back angrily.

"Right!" Toni responded, her temper flaring now. Might as well let it all out, she thought recklessly. This is the last time I'll ever talk to him. "What I want is plain, old-fashioned marriage. I want a home and kids and a career, too, if I can manage it."

"You want it all."

"Yes, and what's wrong with that? I'm willing to give a hell of a lot in return. Oh, Theo, I'm willing to give everything I'm asking for . . . love, support."

"What you want is a damn royal romance like you covered in London. A wedding in a cathedral and an archbishop saying 'Till death do you part.' You want a guarantee of living happily ever after!"

"You get a guarantee with a dishwasher, not a marriage!" Toni responded furiously. "I think you're more hung up on guarantees than I am. But you're right about the rest of it. I *do* want to promise to love someone forever. Maybe I won't make it, but I'm damn sure not afraid to try. And from now on I'm not settling for anything less."

"Good luck," Theo said with an awful finality. "You're going to need it."

Just then the agent announced the final boarding call for the flight to New York.

For one mystical moment, Toni stood rooted to the spot. She almost felt as if she were under a spell. If she could stay perfectly still, perhaps nothing would happen. Perhaps she could stop time and undo what she had just done. She knew when she moved the spell would be broken and she would have to go forward into a life that didn't include Theo.

Then a tear rolled down her cheek and Theo reached down to brush it away tenderly, his anger gone now. The movement broke the spell. She turned and walked resolutely down the jetway without once looking back.

# 17

Theo drove aimlessly up Pacific Coast Highway, with no particular destination in mind. When he passed Toni's empty house he purposefully looked the other way. Vaguely, he considered going all the way up to Carmel and spending the night, but immediately rejected the idea. Being in that romantic, quaint little village would only remind him of Toni. It would be so much more fun, he knew, to see it with her. Somehow, everything was more fun when Toni was around.

She had been gone for a week. And though Theo made a desperate effort to keep himself busy constantly, she was never out of his thoughts. While he worked, while he visited Charlie in the hospital, he thought of Toni. He felt possessed by her memory. At night, it was even worse. He lay in bed, remembering how her tiny, lush body had felt against his, and he ached for her.

Forget her, he told himself repeatedly. But he couldn't do it.

Alone in the car, with nothing else to distract him, Toni's memory haunted him. There were so many things about her that he couldn't put out of his mind . . . the

tender look that came into her lovely eyes when she
kissed him softly after making love . . . her smile, open,
spontaneous . . . her quick mind and delightful wit . . .
the meaning and fullness she brought to his aimless
life. . . .

She had a way about her; a way of making him feel
more a man than Gayle had ever done. A way of making
him feel at peace with himself.

I don't know what it is about her, he thought, puzzled.

But as his hands gripped the steering wheel angrily, he
came face to face with the hard fact that life without
Toni was bleak and lonely and utterly devoid of
happiness. . . .

He didn't realize he was near Santa Barbara until he
saw the sign indicating the exit that led to Leonie Vallis'
ranch. Without making a conscious decision, he turned
off there. When he drove up the curving drive several
minutes later, he saw the fountain bubbling playfully. But
this time there was no rainbow.

The servant who answered the door showed Theo into
the sitting room, then left to tell Leonie of her visitor. He
returned a moment later and informed Theo that Leonie
was in the garden and would see him there. He led the
way outside, then unobtrusively disappeared as Theo
found Leonie.

She was cutting roses, putting them into a basket that
sat at her feet. She wore thick gardening gloves and a
heavy white apron over a lavender jacket and slacks. If
anything, she looked even more vigorous than when he
last saw her. And he marveled once more at her vitality.
She was truly a remarkable woman. Her granddaughter,
he realized ruefully, had inherited more than a little of
that specialness.

"Well, if it isn't Theodopolus Chakiris. Young man,
you're just about the *last* person I expected to see."

"I can understand why," Theo replied, meeting her
level gaze.

"Although Toni didn't tell me the gory details, I understand you two have broken up."

"Did she tell you that *she* left *me?*" Theo asked curiously.

"Yes. But that doesn't really matter, does it? The end result is the same. You did what I asked you not to do. You hurt her deeply."

"Well, I'm not exactly bouncing for joy, myself," Theo said gruffly, admitting openly for the first time how deeply he felt Toni's loss.

"I can see that. You look quite miserable, which I must say is a relief. I half expected you to brush it off like water off a duck's back."

"No. Not that I didn't try."

Leonie smiled then, for the first time. "How about a drink? You certainly look like you could use one."

He followed her back to the house where she set the basket of roses on a table. Taking off her gloves, she shoved them into the pocket of the apron, then hung the apron on a hook by the patio door. She led Theo back into the sitting room, stopping by an intricately carved, heavy oak cart that served as a bar.

"What will you have?" she asked.

"Bourbon," he responded. "Straight."

"I thought so," she said simply, pouring two glasses of fine bourbon whiskey.

"Well, now that my granddaughter has given you what's coming to you, which I suspect no other woman has ever done, what are you going to do with yourself?" Leonie asked, handing him his drink.

Theo smiled drily. "Good question. I *could* continue doing as I've done. I've been very successful, made a lot of money."

"True. But you haven't been happy. Until you met Toni, you were probably too busy running away from yourself to realize that. She made you stop and think, take a good, long look at yourself. You don't like what you see now, do you?"

"What I don't like is the idea of spending the rest of my life photographing death and destruction. And possibly getting killed in the bargain," Theo shot back. He was surprised at how revealing he was being with Leonie. There was something about the old lady that absolutely prohibited small talk and little white lies. He couldn't seem to be anything other than brutally honest with her. And in the process he was being brutally honest with himself for the first time in a very long while.

"You're lucky, you have other options," Leonie said patiently. "You *could* go back to your artistic photography."

"I've been thinking about that," he admitted reluctantly. "In fact, I put together a portfolio of stuff I've done over the years." He smiled ruefully. "But I'm starting from the bottom of the ladder all over again. Right now, I'm just another photographer trying to persuade a gallery to exhibit my work."

"Your work is exceptional, though. You shouldn't have that much trouble."

"Try telling that to the gallery owners I've talked to. They seem to find it quite easy to reject me."

"Where have you been?" Leonie asked curiously.

"Oh, just a couple of places in L.A. I haven't seriously pursued it yet."

Leonie snorted derisively. "L.A. is a vast wasteland when it comes to *real* art. You've got to go to New York."

Theo set down his drink and looked at her soberly. "That would be awkward."

"Why? Because Toni's there? Damn it, Theo, things would be a hell of a lot easier if you'd simply admit you love her and get her back."

"And what if she doesn't want to come back?" he asked, voicing the fear that had been plaguing him on long, sleepless nights. "She's very much your granddaughter, you know. As stubborn and high-handed as they come. She would just as soon shoot me as look at me right now."

"That's true," Leonie agreed ruthlessly. "And I can't say that I blame her. But she loves you, and with her, that's saying a lot. It may be a toss-up whether her stubborn pride or her love for you is the stronger. But you'll never know until you do something about it. What are you afraid of? You've already lost her. Seems to me, things can't get any worse."

"And what about *my* pride? I don't relish the thought of having it stepped on by her."

Looking at Theo shrewdly, Leonie said quietly, "You don't look to me, Theodopolus Chakiris, like a man who's used to taking no for an answer. Especially when it comes to women." Then, while Theo was considering this, she finished in a businesslike tone, "I want to give you a name and address."

She walked over to a nearby desk and sat down. Taking out a pen and slip of paper, she wrote quickly, then folded the paper in two. Rising, she walked back to Theo and handed it to him. "Show him what you've done. If you're as good as I remember you being, he can help you."

Opening the paper, Theo looked at it, then looked back at Leonie. "But he's in New York."

Leonie merely smiled.

# 18

Toni was finishing the broadcast of the morning news show in the big network studio on West 57th Street. Though she had been at work since 5:00 A.M., she looked fresh and exuberant in a lavender tweed suit. As the technicians, cameramen, lighting and sound experts performed their jobs just out of camera range, Toni looked into the camera and narrated a poignant story about adoptees looking for their birth parents. When she was through, the camera switched to her male co-anchor, who gave a brief rundown of the next day's stories. And then the show was through for one more day.

Unhooking her microphone, Toni walked over to Carol, who was standing just off the set.

"You were terrific," Carol said enthusiastically.

"Your story was terrific," Toni responded happily. After only six weeks on the job, she had settled into a smooth routine. She loved what she was doing and was gratified at the fact that she was successful.

"Guess who's in town?" Carol asked, grinning happily.

For one heartrending moment, Toni thought she

meant Theo. Then she realized that Carol wouldn't be so transparently happy if it was Theo she was referring to.

"Who?" Toni asked, pulling herself together. Even now, after all these weeks, the thought of him could still shake her.

"Charlie! He called me last night and he wants us both to have lunch with him today."

"Oh, Carol, don't feel you have to include me. You know what they say about two's company . . ."

"Don't be ridiculous. He's dying to see you."

"So how are things with you two, anyway?" Toni couldn't resist asking slyly.

"Well . . ." Carol let the word drag out suggestively. "Let's just say there are definitely possibilities." Then, more seriously, she went on, "He's a nice guy. A few years ago I would have found that boring. Now, I find it very appealing. It isn't like what you and Theo had, of course," she said frankly. "That kind of grand passion only comes around once in a lifetime, I think. But it's . . . nice."

Toni smiled warmly, genuinely glad that Carol might finally have found the happiness that had always eluded her.

As for her blunt comments about Theo—well, Toni thought sadly, it's true. What we had together was a marvelous, rare thing. It will never come again.

"Listen, I've got some things to do before lunchtime. Why don't I meet you at the restaurant, Le Relais?"

"Okay. I'll come a few minutes late so you and Charlie can have a little time alone."

Carol started to protest, then thought better of it. "Okay. But don't be too late, kiddo."

Two hours later, Toni was stepping out of a cab near the restaurant. In mid-February New York was bitter cold, the streets covered with snow. Toni was dressed warmly in tan corduroy knickers and a wool cape in a rich red, tan and violet plaid.

The restaurant on Madison Avenue was a headquarters for the international set. It was filled to the bursting point with men wearing club ties and chic jogging outfits, and women in suede and leather. The atmosphere was strictly Parisian bistro, a place where the waiters and bartenders joked and mixed with the customers.

Even in this exclusive setting, heads turned to look at Toni as she strode in, looking impeccably groomed and completely self-confident. She was the latest sensation in network news, already being touted as the new Barbara Walters. Her success at her high-powered job and a whole new wardrobe of exquisite clothes had given her a patina of sophistication. But there was something about her irrepressible flame-red curls and the wry amusement in her violet eyes that indicated she was the same unpretentious Toni underneath.

When she reached a table in the corner, Charlie rose and gave her a big bear hug, while Carol looked on happily.

"Toni, you look fantastic," he said, grinning.

"Oh, Charlie, it's so good to see you again," Toni responded sincerely, kissing his cheek and smiling at him warmly.

Giving her a rapid once-over glance, he continued as they sat down, "You look like you just stepped out of Bloomingdale's."

"She did," Carol laughed. "Those are part of her work clothes and they come from Bloomingdale's."

"At home I still prefer faded jeans and a T-shirt," Toni added, laughing.

"Ah, you can take the girl out of California but you can't take California out of the girl," Charlie commented.

They all laughed and Toni reached over to squeeze Charlie's hand. "I really meant it. It is so good to see you. How are you doing?"

"You mean, how's my old war wound?" he asked

impishly. "I've gotten a lot of mileage out of it, actually. When I meet someone new, I manage to drop into the conversation at some point, 'by the way, when I was wounded in El Salvador.' It always impresses them."

Toni grinned. "You haven't changed a bit, have you?"

"I've lost a little weight."

"*Very* little," Carol commented drily. "He spent some time recuperating in Hawaii after getting out of the hospital. And I suspect all he did there was eat."

"Well, the doctor *did* tell me to take it easy," Charlie said, grinning.

"Well, obviously, it worked. You look terrific."

"Not as terrific as you do, Toni. Success agrees with you."

Perhaps, but it isn't everything, she thought sadly.

Her exciting job couldn't fill the emptiness left by Theo's departure. Nothing, she knew, could do that. The dull pain that could flare acutely at the oddest times was something she had grown accustomed to. It was something, she had decided pragmatically, she would have to learn to live with.

"Well, what are you doing with yourself nowadays?" Toni asked, trying to remove her thoughts from Theo.

"Oh, getting various projects going. None of them involve war or foreign travel. I've decided to settle down. I've been looking for a townhouse in Manhattan."

"Oh, Charlie, I'm so glad to hear that. There's a place for sale on my block. Wouldn't it be terrific if we could be neighbors?"

"I'd like that," he agreed, smiling.

"By the way," Carol interrupted, "Charlie wants us to go somewhere with him tonight. You're not busy, are you, Toni?"

"I know it's awfully late notice, but there's an affair I have to go to and I'd like to take both of you."

"Oh, Charlie, I'll just be a fifth wheel," Toni protested.

"Don't be ridiculous," Carol said firmly. She shot a quick, determined glance at Charlie before continuing, "Come on, it will be fun."

Toni wondered what the look that passed between Charlie and Carol was all about. Somehow, she had the feeling that *something* was up, but she couldn't figure out what it could possibly be.

"Well . . ." she began hesitantly. "What is this thing, anyway?"

"Oh, just a new one-man show at a gallery. It's a friend and I've got to make an appearance. It wouldn't take long and afterward we could have dinner."

"Okay, but I've got to make it an early evening. My job gets me up at 4:00 A.M., you know."

"Great. Carol and I will pick you up about six, if that's okay. And it's *very* black tie."

"All right. I'll try to look fancy then," Toni teased.

As lunch progressed, Toni longed to ask about Theo, but she didn't know how to go about it. She tried to think of a way to casually bring Theo into the conversation, but quickly became frustrated. And Charlie wasn't making things easier.

If only he would mention Theo, Toni wished fervently. Then I could say coolly, "Oh, and how is he?"

Finally, when the bill had been delivered and paid, and the conversation was drawing to a close, Toni decided she would have to simply come right out with it.

"By the way, have you seen Theo lately?" she asked, trying without much success to sound only mildly interested.

Charlie looked at her sharply, then said awkwardly, "Well, no, not really."

He's embarrassed, thought Toni, because he knows that Theo and I parted on such bad terms.

Wishing she had never asked the question, Toni said with forced cheerfulness, "Well, I'd better be going. I'll see you two tonight."

As she rose and slipped on her cape, Charlie looked up at her worriedly. "Toni, about tonight . . ." he said suddenly.

"Yes?" Toni asked quizzically.

"Nothing," Carol interrupted firmly, shooting Charlie a quick look.

"Oh. Well . . . bye, Charlie, Carol."

As Toni turned to leave, she caught their reflections in the mirrors that were strategically placed throughout the restaurant. They were looking at each other intently, and their expressions were, strangely enough, worried. . . .

Toni hurried down the long, tree-lined street. Around her, crowds of people scurried home from work. It was five-thirty, already dark and the air was heavy with a biting cold. Yet there was an air of excitement, a symphony of noises, and myriad bright lights. Toni still wasn't used to the loudness and bustle of New York that was in such contrast to the quiet, laid-back style of her life in Los Angeles. There were many times when she missed the peace of her beach house. But she also found New York infinitely more exciting, more exhilarating than L.A.

As she hurried through the crowd toward her apartment building, she glanced at the people around her—the women in heavy fur coats and hats, the purposeful, energetic-looking men. In L.A., these same people would have been casually dressed and would never dream of hurrying to get anywhere. Somehow, New York made these people *want* more, *do* more.

Toni smiled fleetingly as she realized that she, too, had become caught up in the heady drive for success that was so much a part of New York. She enjoyed the fierce competition, and she savored the pleasure of winning. And yet . . .

There is an empty place in my heart that all the excitement, all the success in the world can't fill, Toni thought wistfully as she felt the first snowflakes brush her cheeks. Only Theo can do that. And he is gone forever.

Shaking her head irritably, she tried to banish him from her thoughts, as the doorman opened the wide glass doors to her apartment building.

Toni marched resolutely through the lobby and crammed into the nearly full elevator.

"Good evening, Miss Lawrence," the black-uniformed operator said pleasantly as he maneuvered the controls and the gleaming brass door.

"How are you tonight?" Toni asked politely with the easy familiarity that made her so popular with everyone from the elevator operator to the viewers who watched her on television.

"Fine, thanks, Ma'am. Awful cold tonight, isn't it?"

"Yes, but I like the snow."

"Only someone from Los Angeles could like *this* weather," the man laughed, as he stopped at her floor and opened the door for her.

"Good night, Henry," Toni said, smiling.

As she hurried down the thickly carpeted hall, she glanced at her watch.

I'll really have to hurry, she thought, to be ready in time.

In her apartment, she left her coat on a rack in the tiled entryway, then hurried through the large living room. Determined to make a complete break with her painful past, she had decorated her new home very differently from her old one. The furniture was the same, but it had been recovered in a fabric patterned in a bold navy blue and cherry red. Large, striking modern paintings repeated the color scheme. Huge windows covered with filmy blue drapes led to a small terrace that afforded a magnificent view of Manhattan.

The room was very contemporary, obviously the home of a successful, modern young woman. But as Toni entered the bedroom, the mood changed. Here, she had given in to the romantic in her. In the middle of the room was the Chippendale canopy bed where she had known such profound pleasure with Theo. It was draped now in clouds of silky violet that matched her eyes, with tiny velvet cushions and ruffles and lacy pillows in contrasting shades of violet. In a corner stood a dressing table with a skirt made of the same violet silk. And in front of the small brick fireplace was a wicker rocking chair upholstered in violet.

Barely pausing to glance at the room that she had decorated so lovingly, Toni flung open a closet door and began searching through her evening gowns. Quickly, without giving it much thought, she chose a stunning gown of golden bugle beads over silk organza. Tossing it on the bed, she undressed, leaving her clothes in a muddled heap on the white carpet, and took a quick shower.

Twenty minutes later, her simple makeup and coiffure were done, and she was scrutinizing her appearance in a full-length mirror. The narrow sheath hugged every curve and made her look utterly bewitching. The gown was an expensive Halston original, the first thing she had splurged on after getting her first big paycheck.

As Toni examined her reflection in the mirror, she couldn't help wondering if Theo would like this dress. Wistfully, she imagined what his reaction would be if he were taking her out tonight. Somehow, she didn't care nearly as much what Charlie and Carol might think of her appearance.

At that moment, the doorman phoned to say that Charlie and Carol were waiting for her in the lobby. She asked them to wait, then quickly threw on the white mink cape that Leonie had given her. Enveloped in soft white, with her glistening red-gold hair like a fiery halo above, she looked almost like the angel she had once put atop the Christmas tree as a child.

When she stepped out of the elevator a minute later, Charlie whistled appreciatively.

"Obviously, I'm escorting the two most beautiful women in New York tonight," he said gallantly.

Doing a mock curtsey, Toni said, "Why, thank you, Sir. And may I say, your extremely good manners are exceeded only by your irrisistible charm?"

"You certainly *may* say it," Charlie responded, grinning.

Laughing, Carol said, "Now stop it, Toni, or he'll be impossible all night. Let's get going. We do have a cab waiting, Charles."

The cab ride took fifteen minutes. To Toni's surprise, the closer they got to the gallery on Fifth Avenue, the more quiet and preoccupied Charlie seemed. Toni wondered at first what had happened to his humorous banter, then decided that he probably had a great deal on his mind. He was obviously getting very serious about Carol, and Toni assumed it was that relationship he was thinking about now.

When they pulled up at the curb in typically heavy Fifth Avenue traffic, the gallery was already crowded with splendidly dressed people. The show must be quite a success, Toni thought, as the three of them stepped out of the cab. The "in" crowd of critics, show business celebrities, and the jet set was there in droves. Charlie steered both Toni and Carol through the glittering throng.

Inside, Toni could make out little, at first, of the photographs; only bits and pieces over people's heads and between their shoulders. Intrigued, she looked closer. Then the crowd parted briefly and for one split second she saw the photograph that was the focal point of the show.

It was the photograph of Toni and the little boy in Hyde Park. The child's expression was glowing, rapt, while Toni gazed at him wistfully. Above the photograph was the legend, "Theodopolus Chakiris—The Many Facets of Love."

Stricken, Toni stood rigidly for a moment. Finally pulling herself together, she turned to tell Charlie and Carol that she didn't find this at all amusing. But they were gone. In their place, stood Theo.

He looked the same, heartrendingly so. His eyes were still the deepest, brownest, most compelling she had ever seen. The half-smile that lit his face was still an irrisistible mixture of toughness and sensitivity. She still felt her heart melt as she looked at him. And she still wanted to bury her head in his broad chest and feel his arms enfold her protectively.

But if he was the same, she wasn't. Painful as it had been, she'd learned to live without him these past six weeks. She knew what she wanted out of life and knew he would never give it. She wasn't about to go back to the relationship she'd had with him, despite all the ecstasy it offered.

Something in her look told him how she felt.

"I missed you," he said softly, tentatively.

At that moment they might have been the only people in the room, for all the notice either paid to the milling crowd around them.

"There's nothing more to say, Theo," Toni responded, her voice breaking with an almost unbearable sense of loss.

Seeing the hurt look that came to his eyes, Toni immediately wanted to erase it, to kiss him and make everything all right. But she held back, and instead finished firmly, "Good-bye."

As she brushed past him, their hands touched, and the feeling from that brief contact was electric, as if the ends of two live wires had come together. But Toni forced herself to walk on proudly, her head erect, her gaze steady.

She was out on the sidewalk, looking for a cab, when suddenly she felt familiar arms around her. And the next thing she knew he had picked her up and was carrying her as he used to, easily, in his strong arms.

"Put me down!" she demanded furiously.

"Not till we've talked," he said calmly.

As the crowd on the sidewalk stared at them curiously, Toni lowered her voice. Though her tone was softer, the words were no less angry. "I have *nothing* to say to you! And if you think you can carry me off like some caveman, you're wrong!"

"I was hoping you'd see it more in the lines of a Prince Charming scooping up his lady love in a fairy tale."

His tone was light, glib, unmoved by her fury.

His composure was all the more infuriating as Toni squirmed in his powerful embrace. "Let me go!" she insisted.

He had crossed Fifth Avenue, maneuvering through the densely packed cars and yellow cabs skillfully. They were just entering Central Park now, with its bare, bleak trees standing somberly against the snowy ground. They passed a hot-dog stand covered by a bright umbrella, the hot box steaming in the cold air, the vendor so bundled up that his face was barely visible beneath a heavy muffler and cap.

"I said, let me go!" Toni repeated furiously.

"Okay," Theo agreed suddenly, surprising her. But instead of letting her down on the ground, he lifted her into a waiting hansom cab.

"Ready, Sir?" the driver asked politely.

"Yes. Just keep driving. I'll let you know when to stop."

Toni's mind was in a whirl and her heart seemed to be beating fast. As Theo pulled her close to him on the hard leather seat, she didn't resist. She was caught up in the memory of another ride in a hansom cab. Then, they were in Hyde Park, not Central Park. They had just realized they loved each other and they were speechless under the onslaught of that strange, heady emotion.

"I was afraid that all the talk in the world wouldn't get past your damned pride," Theo explained, looking down at Toni lovingly. "So I decided to try something more symbolic." Then, holding her close and bending his face down till it was only a whisper from hers, he finished huskily, "You're my heart and soul. You give my life meaning. Without you there is no joy or pleasure, only a bleak emptiness."

Then, flashing that dazzling smile, he finished, "Is that romantic enough for you?"

Sitting within the circle of his arms, Toni responded, smiling softly, "Not *quite.*"

She waited breathlessly for that one final thing that would bond them to each other forever.

"I love you," Theo finally said easily. "I want to live together in love with you until our lives end."

Toni remembered when she'd repeated those same words from the royal wedding to Theo. Now, reaching up around his neck and drawing his lips down to hers, she repeated his response: "That has a nice ring to it."

Then his kiss took her breath away, as the hansom cab carried them on into the endless night.

*Silhouette Desire*

## Coming Next Month

### Sweet Bondage by Dorothy Vernon

Maxwell Ross had set into motion a plan to avenge his younger brother. But he was wreaking revenge on the wrong woman, as Gemma Coleridge was only too happy to tell him—at first. But soon, too soon, her heart overrode her head. She lost her anger in Maxwell's arms, in the firm pressure of his lips on hers, and dared to dream of a happiness that could last forever with this rugged Scottish laird.

### Of Passion Born by Suzanne Simms

Professor Chelsie McBride was thoroughly acquainted with her subject—the sometimes humorous, sometimes bawdy Canterbury Tales that could make even her students blush. A respected professional in her field, she was no stranger to the earthy side of passion. But when it was introduced to her in the person of Drew Bradford, she realized she'd only been studying love by the book. Drew's sensual expertise brought out the woman in Professor McBride, and his fiery caresses left her aching to make him *her* man.

## Coming Next Month

### Dream Come True by Ann Major

He had seared her innocence with burning desire. Now, six years after their divorce, Barron Skyemaster, superstar, tried to reclaim her. But how could Amber face him after denying him knowledge of his own son—a son he had every right to know? Trapped with him on his sultry Florida island, Amber clung to the secret of the son they shared, until waves of passion swept them away to a paradise which two can only enter as one.

### Second Harvest by Erin Ross

The fields of Kia Ora were all that remained of Alex's past, and Lindsay was bound to honor her husband's memory by taking an interest in the vineyard. The splendor of Kia Ora was captivating, but Philip Macek, its hard-driving owner, held her spellbound. In his embrace Lindsay sipped the essence of sensual fulfillment and the sweet bouquet of forgetfulness. Wine was for remembrance, but the heady draught of their passion had the power to wash away bitter memories, leaving in their place an intoxicating taste of love.

## YOU'LL BE SWEPT AWAY
## WITH SILHOUETTE DESIRE

### $1.75 each

1 ☐ CORPORATE AFFAIR
Stephanie James

2 ☐ LOVE'S SILVER WEB
Nicole Monet

3 ☐ WISE FOLLY
Rita Clay

4 ☐ KISS AND TELL
Suzanne Carey

5 ☐ WHEN LAST WE LOVED
Judith Baker

6 ☐ A FRENCHMAN'S KISS
Kathryn Mallory

7 ☐ NOT EVEN FOR LOVE
Erin St. Claire

8 ☐ MAKE NO PROMISES
Sherry Dee

9 ☐ MOMENT IN TIME
Suzanne Simms

10 ☐ WHENEVER I LOVE YOU
Alana Smith

### $1.95 each

11 ☐ VELVET TOUCH
Stephanie James

12 ☐ THE COWBOY AND THE
LADY Diana Palmer

13 ☐ COME BACK, MY LOVE
Pamela Wallace

14 ☐ BLANKET OF STARS
Lorraine Valley

-------------------------------------------------------

**SILHOUETTE DESIRE,** Department SD/6
1230 Avenue of the Americas
New York, NY 10020

Please send me the books I have checked above. I am enclosing $_____
(please add 50¢ to cover postage and handling. NYS and NYC residents
please add appropriate sales tax). Send check or money order—no cash or
C.O.D.'s please. Allow six weeks for delivery.

NAME _____

ADDRESS _____

CITY _____ STATE/ZIP _____